I've travelled the world twice over,
Met the famous: saints and sinners,
Poets and artists, kings and queens,
Old stars and hopeful beginners,
I've been where no-one's been before,
Learned secrets from writers and cooks
All with one library ticket
To the wonderful world of books.

© JANICE JAMES.

WIDOW'S END

When Lydia Vail's battered body is found in her secluded house in the Cotswold village of Little Chipping, suspicion inevitably falls on her son, for Oliver has disappeared. But Oliver was said to be devoted to his widowed mother, a possessive woman who has made herself far from popular. In his investigation, Detective Chief Inspector Dick Tansey of the Thames Valley Police Force unearths an old and surprising secret — but by the time he is able to identify the murderer, the killer has struck again.

JOHN PENN

WIDOW'S END

Complete and Unabridged

ULVERSCROFT
Leicester

First published in Great Britain in 1993 by
HarperCollins Publishers
London

First Large Print Edition
published February 1995
by arrangement with
HarperCollins Publishers
London

British Library CIP Data

Penn, John
　Widow's end.—Large print ed.—
　Ulverscroft large print series: mystery
　I. Title
　823.914 [F]

ISBN 0–7089–3246–0

Published by
F. A. Thorpe (Publishing) Ltd.
Anstey, Leicestershire

Set by Words & Graphics Ltd.
Anstey, Leicestershire
Printed and bound in Great Britain by
T. J. Press (Padstow) Ltd., Padstow, Cornwall

This book is printed on acid-free paper

1

LITTLE CHIPPING is not the most beautiful village in the Cotswolds. As a tourist attraction it has little to recommend it. Even its main street is long and straggly. A few groups stop to inspect the Norman arch at the entrance to St Matthew's church and the square tower above, but even at the height of summer the village is not bothered by hordes of visitors. This suits those who live there very well.

Their immediate needs are adequately supplied. Apart from the church, there is a general store cum post office, a garage with a couple of petrol pumps and an owner — Steve Overton — who can be relied upon to undertake minor car repairs, and the Ploughman's Arms, which provides an excellent service under the management of Sidney and Rose Corbet.

Admittedly there is no school, no village hall, no cinema and, other than what the pub supplies by way of darts, shove ha'penny and word games, no form of entertainment, though of course each house has its own radio and telly. And the small market town of Colombury is only twenty-five minutes' walk away across the fields and ten minutes by car on the lanes. For those who want more than Colombury can offer, Oxford can be reached by road in under an hour.

Of course, like everywhere else in Britain, Oxfordshire had been hit by the recession, and the village of Little Chipping has its share of unemployed. Among these was Fred Denham who had lost his job as a painter and decorator when lack of business had forced the family firm in Colombury where he had worked for over ten years to make him redundant. He had now been on the dole for twenty-four months and, though he was only in his late thirties, his prospects of getting further regular employment locally seemed negligible. Even the part-time work, odd jobs for some of the bigger houses around, had dwindled to a trickle and then stopped. It was weeks since he had earned enough for a beer.

Sometimes he wondered what would become of him and his family if anything happened to his wife, Meg.

That was what Meg herself was wondering as she cycled through the village. It was eight-fifteen on a beautiful June morning, and Little Chipping still seemed half asleep, but Meg already felt tired. She had been up for some hours, making sure the children — there were five of them — were washed and dressed, giving them their meagre breakfasts, seeing them off on the school bus that would take them to Colombury, each carrying his or her packet of sandwiches for lunch, tidying the cottage, leaving Fred his midday meal. And her working day had only just begun.

Six days out of seven she went out cleaning, scrubbing, washing, ironing, and on the seventh — apart from church — she did the same chores for her own house and family. She was only in her mid thirties, but often she felt sixty. Nevertheless, thankful that she was unable to have another child and that generally the family was all healthy, she usually managed to stay reasonably

3

cheerful. Today was an exception. In the first place, her youngest had been sick in the night, then there had been a lot of grumbling about breakfast, and to cap it all today was Thursday.

Meg hated Tuesdays and Thursdays, because they were the days she went to the Widow Vail's. She arrived at eight-thirty and left at four-thirty. She was allowed fifteen minutes for a mid-morning break and forty-five minutes for lunch; she was paid for seven hours' work. The lunches she was given were inadequate — Mrs Vail had explained that she and her son dined at night — and during the years she had worked there she had never received the smallest gift, not even at Christmas.

Employers varied, Meg knew. They couldn't all be like Mrs Moore, the vicar's wife. Grace Moore always saw she had a hot meal in the middle of the day, sent her home early without docking her pay if she had a cold, and, in addition to such things as eggs or a jar of homemade marmalade or some freshly-baked scones, gave her frequent presents of clothes for herself and her family. Mrs Vail was quite the reverse.

But it wasn't the Widow's lack of generosity that Meg minded. It was her constant watchfulness, as if she were afraid that unless she kept an eye on her Meg might steal a tin of soup or sit down for an illicit five minutes' rest.

Why Meg continued to work for the woman she didn't know, except that steady employment wasn't easy to find these days, especially so conveniently located — just a short bicycle ride to the far end of the village — and she needed the money.

★ ★ ★

Meg turned off the road on to a wide rutted drive that led up a steep incline to the Vails' house. As usual, the sight of it depressed her, though it was not an ugly building. Constructed of the creamy-coloured stone that was quarried in the Cotswolds not far from Little Chipping, it stood four-square and solid in a couple of acres of land. Any estate agent would have been justified in calling it 'a most desirable property'. But it was

5

overshadowed on two sides by woods which, while protecting it from winds and storms, tended to give it a glossy, mysterious appearance.

Meg dismounted from her bicycle half way up the hill, and walked the rest of the way, wheeling her cycle around to the rear of the house. She was propping it against the wall of the utility room when she saw the tie draped over a rhododendron. She stared at it in disbelief.

Her husband Fred only wore a tie on Sundays, when the Denhams went to church. A few weeks ago he had had a birthday, and the children had clubbed together to buy him a new tie, dark blue with red spots, not silk — they couldn't afford that — but a good quality tie nevertheless. He had been pleased with it; his old one was greasy and tired-looking. But now here it was, or one exactly like it, hanging on a rhododendron in Mrs Vail's garden.

Gingerly Meg removed the tie from the bush. It was dry and clean, and it had certainly not been there on the Tuesday; she was sure she would have noticed it. But how had it got there? Fred had no cause to visit the Vails and, even if he had, why should he have worn his tie and then left it behind? As these questions thronged her mind, Meg carefully folded the tie and put it in her handbag.

At the same time she got out the key of the back door. She opened it and went into the kitchen. Automatically, her thoughts still on Fred and his tie, she took off her jacket, put on her apron and changed into the soft slippers she wore for housework. Then, equipped with a feather duster, some cloths and polish, she went along the passage to the sitting-room. She didn't notice the dark stains on the hall carpet.

The door of the sitting-room was ajar. She pushed it open and had taken a step into the room before her brain accepted the enormity of the spectacle that confronted her. The Widow Vail, who seemed to have lost most of her head, lay on her back in a welter of blood, and there was more blood everywhere, on the carpet, the walls, the sofa, the chairs. The curtains weren't drawn and the early morning sun made a path of light across the body and emphasized by contrast the horror of the scene.

Meg didn't scream. For several seconds she covered her mouth with her hand and uttered small whimpering sounds. Then she turned and fled, dropping dusters and polish in her flight. She tore through the kitchen and out of the house. She didn't think to collect her handbag and other possessions. Her one desire was to get away and put as much distance as possible between herself and the dreadful sight in the sitting-room.

She clambered on to her bicycle, laddering a stocking as she did so, and pedalled furiously down the drive to the road. Her aim was to get to the vicarage — there was no police station in Little Chipping — and tell the Moores what she had seen. She knew they would know what should be done and would cope with the situation. She wanted no part of it.

★ ★ ★

In the event she had got no further than half way through the village when she saw the vicar driving his car towards her with his son, Alan, beside him. She waved frantically for him to stop and, in her anxiety, let her foot slip on one of the pedals. The front wheel of the bicycle skittered sideways and she fell, the bike on top of her. Winded, she lay, sobbing for breath, too distressed to make an effort to get to her feet.

Basil Moore's reactions were quick. He had slammed on his brakes and was out of the car before his nineteen-year-old son had undone his safety-belt. Nevertheless, he wasn't the first to reach Meg. Fortuitously she had fallen from her bike directly in front of the Ploughman's Arms. At this time of the morning the pub was closed to customers, but Sidney and Rose Corbet were both in the bar, washing glasses and generally clearing up, and the doors and windows were wide open in order to air the place and get rid of some of last night's liquor fumes.

The Corbets saw the whole thing and reached the scene first and together. They extricated Meg from her bicycle, which had a badly bent front wheel and, while Alan propped the bike against the pub wall, Sidney with Basil Moore's help carried the injured woman into the bar and laid her on a banquette. In spite of the fact that she worked extremely hard and ate sparingly Meg Denham was no light weight. The fall had been heavy and for the moment she couldn't speak, winded as well as shocked.

The Corbets, so alike with their fair hair, blue eyes and pink cheeks that they might have been brother and sister rather than man and wife, fussed over Meg, bringing her water and offering her brandy. But it was the vicar's hand to which she clung.

"What's happened?"

The newcomer was Elaine Pulman, the barmaid at the Ploughman's Arms. A pretty girl with big brown eyes and pert upturned nose, she was the object of desire of almost every young man in the district, including, to his mother's annoyance, Alan Moore, who was now ogling her from the doorway. Elaine gave him a wide smile before turning her attention to Meg.

"Meg had a bad fall from her bike," Sidney Corbet said.

"I'm quite sure there's more to it than

that," said his observant wife. "Otherwise she wouldn't have been cycling down the street in her apron and slippers. Very particular about things like that, Meg is."

"Yes, something's wrong," Basil Moore agreed. "She was violently waving to me to stop, which is why she fell off her bike. What is it, Meg? What's the trouble?"

By this time Meg was recovering from the double shock, the appalling sight in the Vails' sitting-room and the nasty fall from her bike. She was among friends. She was shaken and she might have a few bruises, but she wasn't badly hurt; she hadn't broken any bones, which was lucky because Fred and the children would never have coped if anything worse had happened — Then she reproached herself for thinking of what might have happened to her instead of what had happened to poor Mrs Vail.

"It's the Widow," she sobbed. "She's dead."

★ ★ ★

A moment of stunned silence was followed by a babble of questions as

11

to how, when, where, but, although Lydia Vail was not the only widow in Little Chipping, no one asked whom Meg meant. Ten years ago when Mrs Vail had bought the lonely house at the far end of the village and come to live there with her son, Oliver, who had just left his public school, they had been made welcome. The house had been empty for several years and it was hoped that the new residents would patronize local workmen, use the local shop and add to the social life of the place.

These hopes couldn't have been more misplaced. Mrs Vail used painters and decorators from Oxford to restore the house and got most of her supplies of food and drink from there or, failing that, from Colombury. She rarely went into the general store in Little Chipping, and she didn't buy petrol from the local garage. She did employ Meg Denham as a cleaning woman and Vic Rowe as a gardener, but only after a succession of others had been sacked or had left of their own accord. And she never entertained, or took any part in village occasions like the annual church fete, though she attended St Matthew's regularly every Sunday.

None of this, however, had earned her the sobriquet of the 'Widow'. The name, which was not one of affection, arose from the fact that she always wore black, very occasionally in the summer relieved by a touch of white. No one had ever seen her in other colours, and there had been some salacious remarks made in the Ploughman's Arms about the kind of lingerie and nightwear she might favour.

"No, she didn't die in her sleep. She's not in bed." Meg answered the last question she had been asked. "She — she's lying in the middle of the sitting-room carpet."

"Are you sure she's dead, Meg?" Rose said. "Perhaps she's had a faint. Did you touch her?"

"No, I didn't touch her." Meg shuddered. "But she's dead, no doubt of that, horribly dead. Her head's smashed in and there's blood all over the place. That's why I came for help." She began to sob again.

Over her head the two older men

exchanged glances. Then Basil Moore gave a brief nod. Reluctantly he took charge.

"Right! Sidney and I will go along to the Vails' and do whatever is necessary."

"Dad," interrupted Alan, "shouldn't we get on to the police as soon as possible?"

The vicar regarded Meg Denham doubtfully. "I was wondering about that," he said, "but I don't think there's any point in creating a panic or scaring Oliver until we're quite certain what's happened. Rose, I suggest you make Meg a cup of tea and when she's recovered a bit Alan can take her along to the vicarage and Grace will look after her."

"The front wheel of her bike is buckled, Dad. It won't turn," Alan said.

"Won't it? Oh dear! Then you'd better carry it to the garage while Meg's having her tea and see if Overton can straighten it. Will that suit you, Meg? You'll be able to walk the short distance from here to my house with Alan, won't you? I don't want to wait any longer."

"I can go with them," Elaine volunteered. "In case Meg comes over faint on the way."

"That would be great!" Alan was visibly cheered.

"You're all very kind," said Meg. "I'm sorry to be such a nuisance but — Mr Moore, could you bring away my handbag and jacket and shoes. I left them in the kitchen and I — I can't go back for them."

"Yes, of course," Basil Moore agreed at once. "But we'll need to get into the house. What about a key? You must have one, Meg."

Meg clapped a hand over her mouth. "It's in my handbag, Mr Moore. After what I'd seen I just ran. I never thought of locking up. The back door's open. You can get in that way. But be careful, please! He might have come back."

"Who might have come back, Meg?" Basil forced himself to be patient.

"The man what killed the Widow — Mrs Vail. He might have come back to collect his rifle. He'd left it lying there beside her body and it could identify him, couldn't it?"

15

2

THE two men didn't speak until they were in the vicar's car heading for the Widow's house at the end of the village.

Then Sidney Corbet said, "I always thought Meg was a sensible woman, but what on earth can one make of this — body on the carpet, blood everywhere, and now a rifle? Could she have hit her head when she fell off her bike?"

"Even if she did I doubt it would have caused such delusions. I'd think Mrs Vail probably had a stroke or a heart attack and that she hit herself on some sharp object when she collapsed. That would account for the blood. As for the rifle, that could be Meg's imagination. Obviously she was in a state of shock."

"If the Widow is dead what do you reckon Oliver will do? Do you reckon he'll stay on in Little Chipping?"

"Why not? It's a fine house and convenient for his banking job in

Colombury. I'm assuming he'll inherit. He certainly should. He's been a devoted son."

"Too devoted. If you ask my opinion he should have defied his mother years ago and married that attractive little Katie Sorel he's been courting for so long."

Basil Moore had not asked for the publican's opinion. Nor did he wish to hear it. He tried not to gossip about his parishioners, but it wasn't always possible to avoid such conversations, and today seemed to be a special occasion. He could understand Sidney's desire to talk. After all, not all that much happened in Little Chipping, and if the Widow had died unexpectedly it would be a topic of conversation in pub and at church for weeks to come.

"Mind you," Sidney continued, "it would be quite something to take on that child of Katie's. She does rather give one the creeps, though she's pretty to look at, like her mother. Did you know that the Widow called her 'that little loony'? It made Katie furious, for Katie's got a temper though she's such a small woman she looks as if she'd blow away in a breeze."

"Small people are often aggressive," Basil Moore said, and added thankfully, "Here we are."

He drew up in front of the house, and together the two men walked around to the back door, which was open. They entered and at once Sidney pointed to the bloodstained footprints on the carpet.

"Meg's?" he queried.

The vicar shrugged. The footprints were smeared and to him the blood looked dry. But he saw no point in giving an opinion which would merely be a guess. He led the way towards the sitting-room. He had been in the house only once before. He had called on all his regular parishioners soon after he arrived in Little Chipping some six years ago, but Mrs Vail had made it clear that she did not like uninvited visitors and he had not called again.

He reached the doorway of the sitting-room and stopped so abruptly that Sidney Corbet who was close behind cannoned into him. They stood and stared into the room, much as Meg had done. The scene hadn't changed, except that the sun was now shining directly on what had been Lydia Vail's head. It was an appalling sight.

"Christ — " said Sidney, and out of respect for the vicar swallowed the rest of the oath. "Poor woman! Whatever she was in life she didn't deserve an end like this. She can't have been more than sixty." He closed his eyes and leaned against the wall. He felt sick. "We must call the police."

Basil Moore took him by the elbow and steered him down the hall. Until he had been invalided out of the Services as a result of a freak accident the vicar had been an army padre, and this was not the first shattered body he had seen. Nevertheless, he had no desire to dwell upon it.

"Come along, Sidney," he said. "We've wasted enough time already. We should have accepted Meg's word."

"Phone!" Sidney pointed to the instrument on the hall table, that Meg had ignored in her headlong flight from the house.

"No, better not touch anything. We'll

use my car-phone."

"Right."

★ ★ ★

Outside, Sidney straightened his shoulders and took great gulps of the clean summer air. He was slightly ashamed of his reaction to the scene in the sitting-room and was thankful that when he spoke he sounded quite calm.

"This is going to be a blow for Oliver. It must have happened after he went to work this morning."

Basil Moore didn't comment. He merely handed Sidney the telephone directory he kept in his car and said, "Look up the number of Oliver's bank — it's the Midland, isn't it? — while I phone the Colombury police station. I know their number."

While Sidney did as requested the vicar got through to Sergeant Donaldson. Having explained who he was, he said, clearly and bluntly, "One of my parishioners, Mrs Lydia Vail, who lives in the house at the end of the village near the wood, appears to have

20

been brutally killed."

Donaldson was in his third year as head of the constabulary in Colombury, but he was still vague as to the exact location of Little Chipping. Certainly, during the time he had been stationed in the Cotswolds there had been no trouble in that village. But now the vicar was saying some woman had been killed there.

"Do you mean murdered, sir?" he asked.

"I very much doubt if it was an accident."

The sergeant sensed the suppressed irritation behind the remark; he could scarcely have failed to notice it. "Very good, sir. Please give me the details," he said placatingly. "You're at the Vails' house. You've found the body in distressing circumstances, you believe — "

"Sergeant!" The Reverend Basil Moore hadn't forgotten his army days and, when it suited him, he could sound peremptory. He didn't intend to have a long and pointless conversation with Sergeant Donaldson at this stage; he wanted to get hold of Oliver. "I'm

21

reporting what appears to be a particularly nasty killing of an elderly lady. I think it's a serious crime. I suggest you contact the Headquarters of the Thames Valley Police at once. You won't have the resources in Colombury to cope with the situation. Then come out here as quickly as you can."

Having heard the note of command in the vicar's voice, Donaldson capitulated.

"Yes. I'll do that, sir. Right away."

Basil Moore gave Donaldson instructions about how to find Little Chipping and the Vails' house, and agreed to wait until he arrived. Then he turned to Sidney Corbet. Sidney had found the bank's phone number and was pointing at it.

"Would it be best to ask for Mr Clement?" Sidney asked. "He's the manager at that branch of the Midland Bank. I bank there and I know him quite well. He's a nice chap. He could break the news to Oliver tactfully."

Basil Moore thought that it was scarcely possible to tell a man tactfully that his mother had been murdered. Nevertheless, when he got through to the bank, he asked for the manager and explained the situation to him.

"Poor Vail," David Clement said. "Hang on a minute while I ask my secretary to bring him to my office." And after a brief pause he continued. "Who do you suppose it was? A would-be thief whom the unfortunate lady surprised? It's dreadful how much violence there is around these days, even in what used to be a quiet, peaceful countryside." He paused, then said, "One moment. I think he's coming. You'll speak to him yourself, Vicar? It'll come best from you."

By now Basil Moore was half expecting this, and was thinking how to word what he had to say to Oliver. He wished it didn't have to be over the telephone, but was thankful that at least Oliver would be in a private place when he learned the news.

"Vicar?"

"Yes, Mr Clement?" He was mildly surprised that the bank manager had come back on the line.

"Mr Moore, I'm sorry, but Oliver Vail isn't here. He didn't clock in this morning and he hasn't telephoned."

23

"What is it, Vicar? What is it?"

Basil Moore did his best to smile but he knew his expression was bleak. He had tried to suppress his fears, but this was no longer possible. Ever since he had noticed that the blood on the hall carpet looked dry he had suspected that whatever had happened to the Widow had not been very recent — a suspicion strengthened when he saw the dreadful sight in the sitting-room — and he had wondered about Oliver who, he presumed, would normally not have left the house until after eight that morning.

"What is it, Vicar?" Sidney persisted.

Basil found that he was reluctant to tell him, but there was no cause to lie. He was jumping to conclusions which could easily be false. He could be wrong about the colour of the blood, and there could be many reasons why Oliver had not gone to the bank that morning — not that he could think of any.

"Oliver's not at the bank," he said, "and he hasn't phoned."

"You mean he's — missing?"

"Well, no one seems to know where he is at the moment."

"Oh God! You don't think — That would be too awful. Ought we — ought we to look?"

"Look? I don't understand."

"He could be upstairs in one of the bedrooms. Or in the dining-room. The door was shut. He could be anywhere in the house, lying there, dead like his mother."

The publican was visibly upset by the idea and Basil Moore felt reproached. Sidney Corbet who knew Oliver much better than he did and clearly liked him had at once come up with what could be a valid explanation of Oliver's failure to go to work that morning. It was a charitable explanation, and no less likely than that a devoted son should have suddenly revolted against an overbearing mother, killed her and fled. But it was not an explanation, Basil Moore admitted to himself that had occurred to him.

"If you're right, Sidney, there's nothing we can do for him. Better wait for the police, I think. Donaldson should be here soon and, if he's taken my advice, the contingent from the Kidlington HQ won't be far behind."

"As you say." Sidney grinned a trifle sheepishly. "I must admit I'm none too keen to go back to that house to look for a second body, not if it's anything like the poor Widow's. That was a ghastly sight! I don't blame Meg for bolting."

"Nor do I." Basil Moore agreed, his thoughts elsewhere. "Sidney, Mrs Vail owned a big Jaguar, but Oliver rides a motorbike, doesn't he? He used it to go to the bank."

"Yes. It's more convenient than a car. All-day parking's not easy in Colombury. But why do you ask?"

"When we were driving in I noticed that the garage has a window in the front, and I thought you might check if Oliver's motorbike was there. Then at least we'd know if he had set off this morning or not. Would you mind, Sidney, while I phone my wife and make sure Meg's got to the vicarage safely?"

"No, of course not. It's a good idea, Vicar."

"Hello!"

Basil Moore sighed with relief. He liked Sidney Corbet and admired the way he ran the Ploughman's Arms so that it was a social centre for the village, but never a source of violence. Nevertheless, he was glad to be alone for a short while and to hear his wife's calm, comforting voice.

"Grace, it's me. Has Meg Denham arrived at the Vicarage yet?"

"Yes, dear, a few minutes ago, with Alan, and Elaine Pulman. There's just been time for them to tell me their version of what's happened. Are you at the Vails'?"

"Yes. I'll have to wait for the police. It's true, Grace. Mrs Vail has been brutally murdered. That's all we know at the moment."

"How dreadful! Have you told Oliver?"

"No." Basil Moore hesitated. "I can't get hold of him. He's not at his bank and he's not phoned in, so they don't know where he is."

"Good gracious! And, Basil, one other

thing — have you collected Meg's belongings? She's very worried about them, and she said you promised you would."

"No, I haven't. To be honest, I completely forgot them."

"Then do get them. I'll tell her you're going to, and they'll be quite safe with you. It's the handbag she's particularly anxious about."

Slightly reluctantly, Basil Moore agreed. It seemed unkind to refuse, and Meg's possessions, left in the kitchen when she arrived for work, could have no relevance to the crime. But he knew the police would not approve of a return to the house, and the removal of anything, relevant evidence or not. So it was with a feeling of guilt that, having said goodbye to his wife, he left the car and went across to the kitchen.

Meg's jacket was hanging neatly over the back of a chair. Her shoes were underneath and her handbag on the seat. Scooping them up, Basil Moore knocked the bag on to the floor, where it opened and spilled its contents across the tiles. Hurriedly he bent to pick them up, but paused as he saw the tie that had fallen out. It was a man's tie, and he wondered what it was doing in Meg Denham's bag.

He didn't waste time pondering the question. He was out of the house and had reached his car as he heard the sound of a police siren announcing the arrival of Sergeant Donaldson and two police constables. Sidney Corbet was standing by the car and didn't bother to hide his relief at the sight of the vicar.

"I couldn't imagine where you'd gone," he said.

"To collect Meg's belongings from the kitchen, as she asked me." Basil Moore tossed the things into the back of the car. "What about you? Is Oliver's bike in the garage?"

"Yes. The bike's there, but the big Jaguar the Widow used to drive — that isn't."

"I see — or rather I don't." Basil sighed. "But here's Sergeant Donaldson. It's up to the police now."

★ ★ ★

Sergeant Donaldson, who had replaced the cheerful and easy-going Sergeant Court over two years ago as head of the Colombury police station, was the opposite of his predecessor. He was a small, slim, straight-backed man, with a high sense of his own importance. However, he had learnt at least one thing since coming to his present job; seemingly simple cases in the country were often more complex than those in towns and cities, and it was wiser to appeal to his Headquarters early rather than late, when much of the evidence could have been disturbed or obscured. He had therefore not needed the vicar's admonition to contact the Thames Valley Police HQ at Kidlington. He had done that immediately he had taken in what Moore had to say, and now he knew that what he privately thought of as 'back-up' was on its way. Meanwhile, he was in charge and he was determined to show it.

The vicar and the publican told their story. They didn't lie. They didn't prevaricate. But, because of Donaldson's attitude, they volunteered no opinions and confined themselves to the bare facts. It was all that was required of them at this point.

"And you haven't been around the house, you say?"

"No. We have been in the kitchen, the hall and on the threshold of the sitting-room. Nowhere else," repeated Basil Moore, controlling his temper.

"Maybe it would be a good idea if *you* searched the house!" said Sidney Corbet.

It was perhaps an injudicious remark, but Sidney was still acting in the belief, however horrible it might prove to be, that Oliver Vail too had been killed. He refused to consider any other possibility.

"No. We mustn't disturb anything. A proper search will have to wait for the scene of crime team. But I'll certainly take a quick look round. My men are already cordoning off the whole area of house and garden and the road outside," Donaldson said pompously. "Will you please wait here," he added. He made it sound like an order.

Donaldson went into the house, and emerged looking pleased with himself as his constables appeared. The three police officers had a long and seemingly confidential conversation. Basil Moore and Sidney Corbet watched them in silence. Then Donaldson returned to them.

"There's not much doubt what happened. A thief! The bedrooms have been turned upside down. Perhaps Mrs Vail was out in the garden and came in and caught him as he got to the sitting-room. Or perhaps she found him there and he killed her first, and then took what he could from upstairs before he left the house. There are a lot of unemployed around these days who would resort to violence rather than go to prison." Sergeant Donaldson shook his head sadly. "Yes, I'd be prepared to bet it'll turn out to be one of those."

The vicar and the publican both smiled weakly in agreement, but neither of them spoke.

Donaldson continued, "Now, let's get down to the details. Do either of you know anything about Mrs Vail's next of kin?"

The vicar said shortly, "She lived

alone, except for an only son, called Oliver. Whether there are any other relatives, I've no idea. Oliver works in a bank in Colombury — the Midland — and I've tried to get in touch without success. Apparently he didn't appear this morning and the bank has no explanation for his absence."

Donaldson, who was no fool, stared at him. "I see," he said thoughtfully. "That could well put a different complexion on the matter."

"Look," said Basil, "can't we go now? We've told you all we know, and I want to get back to the vicarage, and see how the woman who discovered the body is managing. And I'm sure Mr Corbet wants to get to his pub. It must be nearly opening time."

Donaldson considered for a moment. Then the problem solved itself. The sound of sirens heralded the arrival of the Kidlington contingent. "Just wait till I've had a word with them. Then we'll see."

3

"HERE we are again, Sergeant Abbot. Back in your old territory," said Detective Chief Inspector Richard Tansey. He was feeling particularly cheerful this morning, having learnt the previous day that his wife was going to have another child. "What sort of village is Little Chipping? Typical of these parts?"

"Not really, sir. It's less attractive than most."

Bill Abbot, who had been born and bred in Colombury and whose parents still lived there, spared his superior a brief glance before returning his full attention to his driving. Care was needed in these Cotswold lanes during the summer; you never knew when you might come on a string of cyclists in the middle of the road or a party of hikers or even a stray horse. He hooted gently as they reached a sharp bend.

"You mean it hasn't got a good pub?"

Tansey said, knowing Abbot's weakness for a satisfying meal with a pint or two of bitter.

Abbot grinned. "That's the one thing it does have. The Ploughman's Arms is a great place, run by a couple called Sidney and Rose Corbet. I'm sure you'll agree with me when you get to know it — sir."

Tansey laughed. A tall, lean, good-looking man, approaching forty, he was the opposite of the burly, slightly overweight sergeant in more than appearance. They came from different backgrounds; Dick Tansey's father had been a schoolmaster, Bill Abbot's a greengrocer. Tansey was hardworking and ambitious, while Abbot was content to remain a detective sergeant. And their ideas of a perfect evening, weekend or holiday were completely different. Nevertheless, they got on well together. When Tansey had any choice, he always preferred to work with Abbot and by now, since this also pleased the Sergeant, they had become one of the best teams in the Serious Crime Squad of the Thames Valley Police.

"Here we are," said Abbot a few minutes later. "That's Little Chipping church. I gather we go right through the village, and the Vails' house is the last one on the left before the woods, up a steep drive."

"Fairly isolated, then?"

"Yes. Lonely, I'd think."

But when they reached the house, it seemed far from lonely. On the contrary, it was a centre of activity. There were four cars drawn up in front and a van which Tansey and Abbot knew constituted an 'incident room' whose occupants would be in close touch with their Kidlington Headquarters and its computers. Two men in casual clothes — one of whom Abbot recognized as Sidney Corbet — were helplessly watching a young woman police constable vomit into a flowerbed, and another officer, whom Tansey assumed had been stationed there to keep away the media and any curious members of the public when the news of the crime spread, was at present busying himself with directing traffic. Now he came forward and opened the car door for Tansey.

"Good morning, sir. It seems to be a bad business. Inspector Whitelaw's inside with Dr Band — and the body. Shall I fetch him?" Tansey was glad to hear that Inspector Whitelaw was in charge of the scene of crime team with which he would have to work.

"Yes, please," he said, "or I'll go in, but first tell me who else is here."

"Sergeant Donaldson and a couple of his men from Colombury are searching the garden and the surrounding area." The officer failed to suppress a smile, knowing that the Inspector's intention had been to get Donaldson out of the way. "The photographers and the rest of Inspector Whitelaw's team are busy doing their various jobs around the place, but the pathologist, Dr Ghent, hasn't arrived yet. The two gentlemen over there" — he indicated Basil Moore and Sidney Corbet — "are the ones who called us, though neither of them found the body. One's the local vicar and the other's the publican."

"Right. Perhaps I'd better introduce myself to them while you fetch the Inspector." Tansey turned to Abbot. "Go and find Donaldson, will you? Remember this is his patch, so he mustn't be ignored. But he'll need more help if we're to do a proper search of this garden and those woods. Fix it with Kidlington, will you?"

"Yes, sir," said Abbot. Then he responded to the warning about Donaldson, whom he didn't like. "I'll be diplomatic with the Sergeant," he added.

★ ★ ★

The Reverend Basil Moore had had enough of standing about ineffectually while a buzz of activity surrounded him, and he recognized authority in Tansey. He went to meet him.

"I imagine you're the senior police officer. I'm Basil Moore, the vicar of St Matthew's at the far end of the village. We were asked to wait, though we've told Sergeant Donaldson all we know. I need to get back to my vicarage, and Mr Corbet here needs to get back to his public house. Incidentally, Mrs Denham, who found poor Mrs Vail, and is suffering from shock, is at present being cared for by my wife."

Tansey, who could understand Basil Moore's impatience and had already appreciated something of the situation, bowed his head in acknowledgement. "Detective Chief Inspector Tansey," he said mildly. "Really the first thing I should do, before I let any witnesses go, is inspect the body, but I'll make this a special case. By all means go now, if you wish, but keep the woman who found the body with you. I'll be along later to talk to her and to you and the Corbets and anyone else who might be of help."

"Thank you, Chief Inspector," said Moore, and started to turn.

Tansey held up his hand. "Just two questions first, please. Did Mrs Vail live alone? And do you know who is her next of kin?"

As he happened to be looking in Corbet's direction he saw the publican's expressive face become tense. However, after a fractional pause, it was the vicar who answered, his voice neutral.

"She had an unmarried son, Oliver, and he lived with her. He works in the Midland Bank in Colombury, as I told

Donaldson. I did try to phone him there, but he hadn't come in this morning."

"Thanks," said Tansey, thinking that there would be plenty of time later to ask more about Oliver.

It was more important for him at the moment to view the body and speak to Dr Band, the police surgeon. Tansey valued Dick Band's opinion. He had always found him pleasant to deal with, intelligent and reliable, and he knew he would be sorry when Band's imminent retirement took place.

He entered the house gingerly, greeting the scene of crime officers at work and noting the bloody footprints ringed with chalk marks on the hall carpet and on the stairs. He found Band preparing to depart.

"A shocking business, this!" Dick Band said without wasting words on greeting. "I've seen some nasty things in my time, but this is one of the nastiest. The man must have gone berserk."

"Man?" Tansey queried.

"A fair assumption. Mrs Vail may have been in her sixties but she was a tall, strong woman and she'd have resisted an attack. Of course, you've not really looked at the body yet?"

"No, but now I see what you mean." Tansey went further into the sitting-room. He was glad to see that all possible bloodstains had been protected. He gave Whitelaw a good mark. But Maurice Whitelaw, he knew, was an excellent police detective, careful, hard-working — and he had brains; if he lacked any quality that might stop him from getting to the top of his profession it was imagination. Tansey smiled to himself; he had himself been accused before now of being over-imaginative.

"How was she killed?" he asked the doctor.

"I don't know. That's the trouble. I've disturbed her as little as possible, but it's clear she was shot — you see the rifle lying on the carpet beside her — and that would have been enough to do for her, but she could equally well have been battered to death first. Ghent may be able to tell you after the post-mortem; I'm told he's on his way. All I can say at the moment is that in my opinion she's been dead for at least twelve hours and probably not more than eighteen. But that's a wild estimate, of course."

"Really?" Tansey was surprised. "If that's true it means she was killed yesterday evening." He thought of Oliver Vail, but didn't comment.

Band said, "I really ought to wait and have a word with Ghent, but I must get back to my surgery. Anyway, here he is. Here's the expert," he added not too kindly as he looked through the window and saw Dr Ghent's expensive Mercedes draw up. "I'll see him on my way out, Tansey. Maybe he'll tell me I've got it all wrong. Not that I think he can do much till he gets her on the slab."

Tansey laughed and lifted a hand in farewell. He knelt beside the body for a moment, considering, and noted that the rifle was itself covered in blood. Then he went back into the hall to meet the pathologist, who was being ushered into the house by Inspector Whitelaw, grumbling as usual that having to see the body *in situ* was a waste of valuable time.

"It's not a pretty sight," said Tansey, who was used to Ghent and had learnt that one got more out of him if one accepted his high opinion of himself rather than tried to ride him.

"Few of them are," said Ghent, "though I admit that some are worse than others."

The three men went into the sitting-room. "Apart from protecting the blood-stains, we've left this room severely alone, sir," said Whitelaw, "until you and Dr Ghent could see it. I'm not even sure if that rifle's been fired, though there was a slight smell of cordite in the room when we first arrived. It's an old army .303, obviously."

"No sign of the round?"

"Not so far, sir, though I think at close range it would have gone right through her head and should be somewhere. We'll search carefully later."

In the meantime Ghent was standing beside the Widow's body. The protection of the bloodstains had made the scene in the sitting-room less appalling than when Meg Denham had seen it. Nevertheless, the colour had drained from Ghent's face and he was wetting his lips with his tongue. Tansey stared at him, amazed.

He had seen the pathologist dissecting dead bodies, with as much indifference as if he were dissecting a rabbit. But now he appeared overcome.

"Are you all right, Dr Ghent?" Tansey asked.

"Yes. Sorry. Stupid of me." Ghent didn't often admit to a weakness. "It was a trick of the light. A ray of sun must have hit the window and been reflected off that mirror on to the body." He pointed to a gilt-framed oval mirror on the wall. "I realize now what happened, but — Christ! — for a second I could have sworn that — the thing moved, was still alive."

"Horrible!" Tansey did his best to sound sympathetic. "How would you say she was killed?"

"It's a guess, but I'd say battered with the rifle until she was senseless and then shot for good measure, perhaps because she recognized him, and he wanted to make sure she was dead. But I repeat, Chief Inspector, as you know full well, that's only guesswork. You'd do far better to wait for my report after the PM."

Tansey didn't comment that it wasn't always possible to wait for the report, and sometimes guesswork could help. He was glad that Ghent had recovered his composure and was back to his old form. The pathologist touched the body and moved an arm gently. "You're going to ask when, aren't you?" he said.

"Yes," said Tansey bluntly.

"Possibly about fifteen hours." Ghent stood up. "Now, there's nothing more I can do here. Get the body to the mortuary as soon as possible, with samples of carpet and upholstery and any other bloodstains around the place."

"Of course," said Tansey, "I gather there are plenty upstairs and in the cloakrooms. Do you think there's any chance of finding the bullet in the body?"

"In that mess?" He pointed at the head and echoed Whitelaw's view, adding, "You'd better look around the room."

Tansey escorted the pathologist to his car, duly admired the new Mercedes, and with some relief watched him drive away.

★ ★ ★

45

Inspector Whitelaw took Tansey around the house. The Chief Inspector had already seen the hall and the sitting-room. Now he was shown the downstairs cloakroom where there were bloodstains in the washbasin and on a towel. There was no sign that either the dining-room or the study had been entered, or of any blood on the rest of the ground floor. But there were bloody footprints on the stairs, in a bathroom, and two of the bedrooms, both of which had obviously been searched quickly and carelessly. Drawers had been pulled out, cupboards opened and, in what appeared to be Oliver Vail's room, clothes were scattered on the floor.

"There's something odd about the whole affair, sir," volunteered Whitelaw as they went downstairs again. "Why did the man wash twice? Why was he only interested in Mr Vail's clothes, which look fairly ordinary to me? Why did he ignore Mrs Vail's beautiful mink coat? Why did he leave his rifle behind? Why did he disregard the dining-room, where there are usually goodies in the way of silver to be found?"

"Those seem enough questions to be going on with," Tansey said as Whitelaw paused to draw another indignant breath. "Let's be positive. What do you think this character *did* take?"

"I can't be precise, sir, because I've no means of knowing what's missing, but I'd say that some of Mrs Vail's jewellery has gone and some cash. Her jewel box and her handbag have both been upended. And possibly some of Mr Vail's clothes, but I could be wrong there. Apart from that, sir, as you see, everything's being photographed and fingerprinted, and we've taken some blood samples for Dr Ghent. We're cutting bits out of the carpets now."

"That's a good effort in such a short time, Inspector." Tansey was always ready to give praise. "What next?"

"I thought perhaps Sergeant Donaldson and his men might do a house-to-house through the village when he's finished searching the immediate vicinity. Sergeant Abbot tells me you sent for some reinforcements for him. Donaldson and his men could ask if any strangers have been seen around lately."

47

"On the assumption that we're looking for a thief who'd been casing the neighbourhood?"

"It's a fair assumption, sir."

"One possibility, certainly. But remember, you heard Ghent say that Mrs Vail was killed yesterday evening. Now, though I don't want to make too much of this, her son Oliver, who lives here, seems to have disappeared. At least he's not at his bank, where he should be at this time of day."

Maurice Whitelaw emitted a silent whistle. "That's interesting, sir," he said softly. "Still, these are early days, and there's no point in jumping to conclusions, as you've often told me."

★ ★ ★

By common consent they strolled outside, and were standing in the sunshine discussing the case, when Sergeant Donaldson, followed by Sergeant Abbot, strode purposefully up to them.

"Chief Inspector, sir — Inspector Whitelaw," Donaldson said, and paused before making his announcement.

"You've found something of interest?" Whitelaw asked drily.

"We've found nothing — and that's what's interesting," said Donaldson, and when the two senior officers looked at him blankly, continued in triumph. "The Vails must have had a car. They were obviously not poor. They wouldn't have used the bus to go shopping, and anyway Oliver Vail went to work daily in Colombury, so he'd have needed one. But there's no car in the garage."

"Was the garage locked?" Tansey asked.

"I — I don't know," Donaldson said.

"Yes, it was, and it's not the self-locking kind, so it must have been locked deliberately," Abbot said, "but it's perfectly possible to see in through a window. There's no car inside, but there is a motorbike, which would have been useful for Oliver going to work, but not much use to old Mrs Vail. Sergeant Donaldson is right, sir. The Vails must have had a car." He looked innocently at Tansey, knowing full well that he had shown up Donaldson not only as incompetent, but prepared to take credit that rightfully belonged to another man.

"Good," Whitelaw said. "We must trace it. We'll need make, year, colour, registration number."

There was a gentle cough behind them and the four men turned. The WPC who had been vomiting into the garden when Tansey and Abbot arrived was standing there. She was a pretty girl with light brown hair and big hazel eyes, but she was still very pale.

"WPC Norton," Whitelaw said. "The officer who's been going through Mrs Vail's desk in the study." He smiled encouragingly at the girl. "What is it?"

"Mrs Vail's car, sir. She bought it six months ago — from the Windrush Garage in Colombury. It's a blue Jaguar. The bill of sale with all the particulars is in her desk."

"That's splendid!" Whitelaw was pleased. "What else? You can't have known we were discussing the car."

"No, sir, I didn't. I came to tell you that Oliver Vail's passport was in the desk, together with his mother's, plus their birth certificates, her marriage certificate — and a firearms licence in

50

her name. That rifle could belong to Mrs Vail, sir."

"It could indeed! Anything else of immediate interest?"

"There was a copy of her will, sir. It gives her solicitor's name and address in Oxford. I glanced at it and it's very simple. It leaves everything to her son."

"Right!" said Tansey. "That's fine, Constable. I want all those confidential papers and any photographs of Oliver you can find. Bring them to the Incident Van."

"Yes, sir."

Whitelaw turned to Tansey. "She'll be good, that girl, once she's learnt not to throw up at the sight of ghastly bodies."

Tansey grinned wryly. "They take some getting used to," he said, and was reminded of the pathologist's odd behaviour. "Anyway, Inspector, you're going to be busy. We'll leave you to it. As you suggested, Sergeant Donaldson, with his local knowledge, is the best man to make house to house inquiries." He hoped Donaldson would accept this as a compliment and feel placated. "In the meantime Sergeant Abbot and I will go and start interviewing the main witnesses. All right?"

"Fine, sir," said Whitelaw, and Donaldson gave a stiff nod as if the question had been addressed to him too.

4

"DON'T ever do that again, Sergeant Abbot," said Tansey as they drove down to the village.

"Do what, sir?"

"You know perfectly well. You made a fool of a fellow officer in front of others, especially a junior. WPC Norton almost certainly heard what you said, and you can't blame her if she repeats it. I'm aware that you don't like Sergeant Donaldson, but you have to work with him. Accept it. You understand?"

"Yes, sir."

Bill Abbot knew that he deserved the rebuke. Nevertheless, he had been surprised by its severity. He hadn't expected the Chief Inspector to treat the matter so seriously. Tansey wasn't apt to be over-punctilious and pull rank, and he had been in such good spirits earlier that morning. Something, Abbot thought, had put him in a black mood.

Abbot was not to know that what had upset Tansey was the sight of WPC Norton, for the girl had instantly reminded him of his ex-wife, and he had realized that their daughter, whom he had not seen for years, would by now have been almost the same age as the WPC. Not that his ex-wife and her present rich husband would have allowed the girl to join the police force. It had been the police force, with its long and uncertain hours of work, that had contributed to the break-up of his first marriage.

He suppressed a sigh as Abbot turned on to the road and said, "Stop at the Ploughman's Arms. It's on the way. And we'll have a talk with the Corbets first. Try to get it over before opening time, so as not to inconvenience them too much."

"Yes, sir," said Abbot meekly. "Here it is."

★ ★ ★

Sidney Corbet had been on the lookout for them. He opened the side door of the pub and showed them into a small family living-room behind the bar, where they were joined by Rose, and by Elaine Pulman who had returned from the vicarage. Introductions over, Sidney offered the two police officers a drink which Tansey, to Abbot's regret, refused, saying it was a bit too early for them.

"Instead, tell us what you know of Mrs Vail," Tansey said, surprising them. "Did you like her?"

"We scarcely knew her," Rose said carefully. "She never came into the bar and she never bought her wines and spirits from us. For that matter, no one in the village really knew her. She kept herself very much to herself."

"Did she have any relations or friends to stay?"

"I don't think so."

"It must have been hard on her son?"

"Bloody awful for him," said Elaine, who had been eyeing Tansey with interest.

"Elaine!" Sidney said sharply.

"Oh, for Heaven's sake! These are the police. There's no point in trying to deceive them. The Widow was an old bitch. We all know that. She made Oliver lead an awful life. She was one of those possessive mothers who think of no one but themselves. And she was only sixty-odd. She wasn't ill. She was perfectly active. She could drive her car. OK. She didn't believe Katie was good enough for him, but she might have asked herself if he was good enough for her. Katie's a good girl. She — "

"Elaine!"

This time it was Rose, and unexpectedly she had more effect than Sidney had done. There was silence. The two Corbets looked at each other, embarrassed. Elaine opened her mouth, but Tansey forestalled her.

"Who is Katie?" he inquired.

"Katie Sorel," Elaine said sulkily. "She's Oliver's girlfriend. He should have married her ages ago, but he was too much under his mother's thumb and the Widow didn't approve, Katie being divorced and that." Elaine didn't seem to realize that she had produced an excellent motive for Oliver Vail to rid himself of his mother.

"I expect I shall be meeting Mrs Sorel

before long," Tansey said. "Where does she live?"

"In Colombury," Sidney said. "She's got a cottage in Green Lane."

"I know it, sir," Abbot said as Tansey glanced at him.

"Good. Then let's forget Mrs Sorel for the moment and return to Mrs Vail. Incidentally, why do you keep referring to her as 'the Widow'?"

Rose hesitated. "Because she always wore black," she said at last. "It was all right when she came here ten years ago just after her husband died, but it seemed a bit much to stay in mourning all this time."

"I see," said Tansey, who didn't. But he let the subject drop. "Now, we've heard Miss Pulman's opinion of her. I think it was you, Mrs Corbet, who said that no one in Little Chipping really knew her, but was she generally liked or disliked?"

It was Sidney Corbet who replied. "Well, she wasn't over-popular, Chief Inspector. Elaine's right in one respect. Nobody likes to speak ill of the dead, but there's no point in trying to mislead you. She was a mean woman, as others will confirm. For instance, she's given poor old Bert Bilson notice to get out of a cottage she owns because he's behind with his rent."

"It's a dreadful place, too," said Rose. "No more than a hovel, but he's lived there for years and God knows where he'll go."

"Perhaps he won't have to go anywhere now Mrs Vail's dead," Sidney said.

"Maybe not, Sidney, but don't be suggesting he might have battered her to death so as to stay in his home," Rose rebuked her husband. "He wouldn't have had the strength, Chief Inspector," she said to Tansey.

Tansey nodded, but he added Bert Bilson to his mental list of possible suspects. If Lydia Vail had been shot first it wouldn't have needed much strength to batter her dead or dying body.

"That cat business was more in his line," Elaine said," suddenly laughing. "I bet it gave the old witch a shock."

"What cat business?" Tansey asked, blessing the irrepressible girl who was giving him so much information, worthless though some of it would undoubtedly prove to be.

"We don't know it was Bert," Rose said, after exchanging glances with her husband, "though I admit he was suspected because it happened just after he'd been given notice."

"What happened?" Tansey asked again.

Sidney answered. "A dead cat, horribly mangled, was put on the Widow's — Mrs Vail's — front doorstep. Nobody claimed the cat, though Oliver asked around. It was probably an unwanted farm stray, run over by a car."

"Or caught in one of Bert's traps," said Elaine.

Abbot saw Tansey's momentary puzzlement, and said, "Bert's a poacher, is he? Supplements his old age pension with a few birds, does he?"

"Mostly rabbits," Sidney said, "up in the woods. Bert insists they're public property, but at least some of the land technically belongs to the Vails, and the Widow called it trespassing. It was possibly another reason she wanted to be rid of him."

"And who else has a grudge against

her?" Tansey asked.

He looked in turn at the Corbets and Elaine. They shook their heads and he tried a different tack, though without much expectation of learning anything of value. But the violence of the crime worried him. If, as seemed probable, the rifle had belonged to Mrs Vail, her assailant must have wrested it from her, but after that his behaviour hadn't been rational. Once he'd shot her in the head, he'd have had no need to batter her body so brutally. On the other hand, if he had battered her first her wounds must have been such that he'd have had no reason to shoot her. It didn't make sense, and Tansey liked things to make sense.

"What about this for a question, then?" he said. "Is there anyone in the village, in the district, who is perhaps a little unbalanced and inclined to bursts of violent uncontrolled temper?"

The Chief Inspector waited for three heads to shake again. Instead they were still, unnaturally still, and he sensed that somehow he had touched a nerve.

"No!" Elaine said firmly at last.

"There's no one like that in Little Chipping or anywhere around."

She looked Tansey straight in the eye, her face bright with innocence, and he knew she was lying, in spite of her protestations about attempting to deceive the police. But the Corbets didn't contradict her or volunteer any remarks. Tansey hesitated. He was interested, but he decided not to press them.

He said, "Of course, it could have been the work of a thief whom Mrs Vail interrupted, either someone who saw an isolated house and took a chance, or a professional who has been on the lookout for a place worth burgling. The second would seem the more likely, which is why Sergeant Donaldson is going round the village asking if any strangers have been seen, but I might as well ask you directly." He smiled at them, wanting them to relax.

Suddenly there was a loud banging outside. Sidney Corbet looked at his watch and leapt to his feet.

"It's past opening time and we're never late. Chief Inspector, I must — "

"Of course, go ahead. Open up.

Perhaps Mrs Corbet could spare us a little more time."

"Certainly! Certainly!" There were more bangs and someone was shouting. Sidney was eager to get away. "That'll be Vic Rowe. He's always one of the first, if he's not working. Elaine, you'd better come with me."

"OK!"

Elaine went reluctantly, leaving Rose Corbet with the two officers. Rose was looking anxious, over-anxious, Tansey thought, and he wondered why.

"This must be a quiet village, Mrs Corbet," Abbot said, filling the silence between them. "Do you have much trouble in the pub?"

"No, hardly any. Sidney is very strict. Vic Rowe can be a bit of a nuisance sometimes — as you've just heard — but what young man isn't? He's the local gardener and handyman," she explained, and added as if it was being forced out of her, "He looks after the Vails' garden."

"Then I expect we'll be having a chat with him," Tansey said, thinking that gardeners were usually peaceful men. "Let's return to what we were talking about when we were interrupted — strangers coming into the pub and asking questions, for instance?"

Rose Corbet shook her head. "People sometimes come to look at the church, mostly American tourists, but they pass through. A certain number will stop over to have a drink in a 'quaint English inn', but we're really dependent on local trade. Not just the village, though that's our mainstay, especially at midday. We've made ourselves a reputation in the district. People from the big houses around drop in regularly and bring friends who are staying with them."

Abruptly Rose stopped speaking, aware that because her attention had been focused on what was happening in the bar, she had been talking too much — and inconsequentially. Then there suddenly came a crash of breaking glass, followed by a loud thump and silence. Rose looked desperately at Tansey.

Tansey nodded at Abbot, who got up and started for the door. But almost at once the buzz of conversation from the bar resumed. There was a burst of laughter and Elaine appeared carrying two tankards of beer.

"For the Chief Inspector and Sergeant Abbot," she announced, "with the Ploughman's compliments." She gave them each a wide smile. "Everything's OK out there. Vic arrived a bit drunk, I'm afraid. Anyway, he's quietened down after Sidney allowed him one drink, though he dropped his glass. Anyway, a couple of his pals are seeing him home."

"Thank goodness for that," said Rose, relieved. She turned to Tansey. "Chief Inspector, you were asking about strangers in the district. I don't think there have been any, at least not suspicious ones."

"What about the Smiths?" asked Elaine, laughing and handing Tansey and Abbot their beers. "Mr and Mrs Smith! I bet that's not their real name."

"Elaine!" Rose protested. "They're a perfectly harmless young couple."

"Are they? Most people who come to stay at Mary Gore's only stop for a few days, but the so-called Smiths have been here for over a week. Why? What have — ?"

"Please!" Tansey interrupted. "Who is Mary Gore? And who is this Smith couple?"

It was Rose Corbet who answered. "I'll explain," she said. "You go back to the bar, Elaine. There'll be too much work for Sidney alone. We'll be extra popular today once the news of the Widow's death gets around. I'm afraid, Chief Inspector," she continued as Elaine went, making a face at her behind her back, "in a small place like this the Ploughman's inevitably becomes a centre of gossip."

Tansey nodded his understanding. "Mary Gore?" he prompted.

"She owns that rather attractive little house three doors down from here. She used to be a schoolteacher, but she retired years ago and she and her sister came to live in the village. Then last year Margaret Gore, who was in her late seventies, died, and Mary decided to take in lodgers during the season. I think she was lonely. I don't believe she needs the money."

"And the Smiths have been staying with her?"

"Yes. They're a pleasant young couple — late twenties, early thirties. They've got a car, but they spend most of their time walking. Mary gives them breakfast and supper, and they have pub lunches. One day it rained, and they came in here for sandwiches, and twice they've been in for a drink in the evenings."

"Not exactly suspicious characters," Tansey said.

"Not in the least. Mind you, Chief Inspector, Elaine might be right. Their name may not be Smith. Mary, who's an innocent soul, believes they're on their honeymoon because they always go to bed early. The alternative, that they're not married, doesn't seem to have occurred to her. But anyhow that's none of our business. I'm sure they're not involved with the Widow's death. I doubt if they've ever heard of her."

Rose looked at her watch. The sounds from the bar had increased in volume, and it was obvious that she wanted to join her husband. Tansey finished his drink and signalled to Abbot to do the same. They both stood up.

"We must be off, Mrs Corbet. I don't

think there are any more questions at the moment. Many thanks for all the help you and your husband have given us. We're very grateful. In a case like this it's essential to learn about the back-ground and the people involved, innocent or otherwise, as I'm sure you — "

His words trailed away as the door from the bar burst open and Elaine came in, her eyes shining with mischief. "Quick, Chief Inspector! Quick! They're going. The Smiths. They're loading their bags into the car right now. Unless you hurry they'll be off and it won't be easy to trace two Smiths, will it?"

She was obviously so intent on causing trouble for the Smiths that Tansey would have liked to ignore her, but he knew it wasn't possible. The couple were probably completely irrelevant to his inquiry, but he couldn't take the chance of letting them disappear. He had to know where they were going, just in case one or other of them might unknowingly possess a vital piece of information.

"Many thanks, Miss Pulman," he said, keeping his voice neutral. "Indeed, thanks for all your help."

He went past her, smiling at Rose, to the side door which Abbot was already holding open for him.

* * *

When the two police officers reached the Smiths' car, which was a five-year-old Ford hatchback that had seen better days, the girl was clambering into the back seat, trying to make herself comfortable among the bags, while the man sat impassively behind the wheel. It didn't require the sight of their angry, set faces to warn Tansey that they had quarrelled and were both in bad tempers.

"Mr Smith?" Tansey inquired politely.

"Yes. Who are you? What do you want? We're in a hurry," Smith said rudely.

"Chief Inspector Tansey." He showed his warrant card. "Will you please get out of the car. I want to ask you a few questions. As I expect you know, there's been a brutal murder in the village and you might be able to assist us."

"You too, madam," said Abbot, opening

her car door and helping her on to the road.

"Perhaps you'd give us some proof of your identity," Tansey said. "I understand you're strangers here."

Smith produced his driving licence and a letter addressed to him. His name was Paul Smith and he lived in Oxford. Tansey memorized the address and handed the documents back to him. He looked at the girl.

"This is absurd," she said. "We've never met the old woman who was killed. We'd not even heard of her until this morning, when our landlady told us about her. She — Miss Gore, that is — had heard the story at the village store."

"I see," said Tansey. "And you are?"

"My wife," said Smith.

The girl turned and glared at him. "I am not your wife and I'm not going to be, Paul Smith, not after the way you've been flirting with that barmaid." She reached into the car for her handbag and extracted a diary which she opened at the Personal Notes page and handed to Tansey. Her name was Patsy Brean,

Mrs Kenneth Brean, and she lived in Woodstock.

"Thank you," said Tansey, returning the diary. "Now, can you tell me what you did yesterday evening?"

"Supper was at six-thirty," she said. "High tea, really. Then I went straight to bed. I had a headache."

Tansey nodded. "And you, Mr Smith?"

"After the meal, I went for a walk — along to the church and beyond."

"So you were nowhere near the Vails' house at any time in the evening?"

"No."

Tansey didn't comment on the fact that Smith evidently knew where Mrs Vail lived. "Well, I think that will be all then. Many thanks for your cooperation. Good morning."

"Good morning," Abbot echoed.

But neither Mr Smith nor Mrs Brean responded.

5

BUSY talking to the 'Smiths' neither Tansey nor Abbot had noticed a small, trim, boyish figure hurrying along the road towards the Ploughman's Arms. Even had they done so, there was no reason for them to have been especially interested. It was not until they had watched Mr Smith and Mrs Brean drive away from Little Chipping in mutual dislike, and were returning to their own car, that they became aware of the young woman on the forecourt of the pub talking to Elaine Pulman.

But Elaine had seen them. She began to wave. "Chief Inspector! Chief Inspector!"

Tansey gritted his teeth. "Damn that girl," he said with feeling.

"She's been quite useful to us, sir," Abbot reminded him.

"I know. Full of helpful information, but frankly I find her a little overpowering."

Abbot, relieved that he was in favour

again after the incident with Sergeant Donaldson, grinned. "She's a bit of an extrovert all right, no respecter of persons, I'd say, dead or alive. I wonder what she's got for us now."

"We'll soon know. Here she comes."

Elaine was approaching fast, her long legs outdistancing her companion. She greeted them with, "You'll never guess who this is, Chief Inspector. It's Katie, Katie Sorel — Oliver's girlfriend." Then she proceeded to introduce the two officers as if they were old friends of hers.

Seen close, Katie Sorel's resemblance to a slim boy was not so marked, though with the right make-up she could have played such a part on the stage. She was not more than an inch over five feet and slightly built, with short dark hair and blue eyes, a pretty woman, except that today she was whey-faced, her brow creased in a troubled frown.

"Chief Inspector, have you found Oliver yet?" she asked without preamble.

"Not yet, Mrs Sorel."

"I came over as soon as I heard Oliver was missing."

"Yes. How did you — "

"I phoned her," said Elaine. "I thought she ought to know. After all, she and Oliver are hoping to get married."

"Unless something's happened to him," said Katie, and added unnecessarily, "I'm so worried. Chief Inspector, have you searched everywhere around?"

"It's being done," Tansey promised. "But there's no reason to believe anything untowards has befallen Mr Vail. Come and sit in the car and we'll have a talk, Mrs Sorel. I'm sure Miss Pulman's services are needed in the bar. You'd better get back, Miss Pulham, or Mrs Corbet will be after us for keeping you from your duties."

"Yes, I suppose so," Elaine said reluctantly. "Goodbye for now, Katie. I'll be in touch. 'Bye!"

She gave a wide wave of a hand that included both the detectives, and Tansey carefully avoided catching Abbot's eye as he opened the rear door of the car for Katie Sorel. Elaine was irrepressible.

★ ★ ★

Once the two men and Katie were settled in the car, Tansey relaxed and said, "Now, when did you last see Mr Vail, Mrs Sorel?"

"Yesterday evening. Sometimes he'll drop in for a few minutes just to say hello on his way to work, but not this morning. And I don't understand it. He can't have set out for the bank before Mrs Vail was killed, because he never got there. But if he was still at home when she found those thieves he'd certainly have done his best to defend his mother, and he'd have been dead by now, too. Unless — "

"Unless — " Tansey prompted.

"Unless they kidnapped him. Have you thought of that possibility, Chief Inspector?"

"Frankly, no," Tansey said.

He knew that the paroxysm of coughing from which Abbot seemed to be suffering had been caused by a need to suppress his laughter. But, in fact, given that she was starting from a false hypothesis, there was nothing wrong with Katie Sorel's logic.

"I did wonder if they might have come on Oliver in the garden somewhere — getting his motorbike from the garage perhaps — and killed him first, which is why I asked you if you'd searched around for him thoroughly!" She shook her head in bewilderment. "Why do people like that have to kill? Do they enjoy it? They could easily have just tied Mrs Vail up. But Elaine said they had been horribly brutal to her."

"They?" Tansey queried.

"I don't know. Elaine just said 'they', and I assumed there were two. Or was it a gang?"

"We have no idea at the moment, Mrs Sorel. However, there is one thing we are sure of — Mrs Vail was killed yesterday evening, not this morning."

"Yesterday evening? But that's not possible."

"It's confirmed by the police surgeon and the pathologist."

"But it can't be. They must be wrong. Oliver — " She stared at Tansey with a mixture of disbelief and horror as she forced herself to accept what she had just been told; she was not a stupid woman, and she understood the implications. "No!" she said. "No, Chief Inspector, you cannot suspect Oliver. He'd be the last person in the world to do his mother any harm. Everyone'll tell you he was devoted to her."

"Please, Mrs Sorel. I'm not accusing Mr Vail of anything, but naturally I would like to find him. You say you saw him yesterday evening. What time was that?"

"He arrived a few minutes after four-thirty. I live around the corner from the bank where he works. And he left at twenty to six."

"You sound very sure."

"I am, Chief Inspector. I turned on the telly for the five-forty news on the commercial channel as soon as he went, and it had just started."

"And about the time he arrived?" Tansey asked, though he didn't think it relevant.

"Yes. I was watching the clock. Tom, my ex-husband had come in. He has a legal right to see our little girl — her name's Joy — and he visits her whenever he's home — to annoy me, not because he loves Joy. He lives with his mother in Colombury but he's mostly away, thank goodness. He's a seaman."

"I see. You were watching the clock because you wanted him gone before Mr Vail arrived?"

"That's right. They don't exactly get on, as you can imagine." Katie smiled ruefully. "Luckily they don't meet very often."

Tansey wasn't interested in Katie Sorel's love-life, except in so far as it involved Oliver Vail. If she were to be believed — and even though she obviously cared deeply for Oliver he had no reason to doubt her — Oliver had an alibi until after five-forty, plus the time it would have taken him to get from Colombury home to Little Chipping.

"So Mr Vail left you at twenty to six yesterday evening. When would he have got home on his motorbike? It must be about a ten-minute ride."

Katie looked puzzled. "Ten minutes? Yes, but — Oliver didn't have his motorbike yesterday."

"You mean he walked to work?" It was Tansey's turn to be puzzled.

"No. He drove Mrs Vail's car — it's a beautiful Jaguar, new and still under guarantee. Mrs Vail thought there was a squeak in the steering wheel, so, as she didn't need it, she told Oliver to take it to Field's garage where she had bought it."

"Field's?" Tansey was sure that wasn't what WPC Norton had said about the supplier of the car.

"Brian Field owns the Windrush Garage in Colombury, sir," said Abbot helpfully.

"Ah, I understand," said Tansey.

"Oliver said she bought it locally because if anything went wrong it was easier to complain and get it fixed," Katie added. "Anyway, that's why he left when he did. He had to go to the garage to collect the car."

"I see. Thank you," said Tansey.

The Chief Inspector was indeed grateful. It would now be possible to verify the time that Vail had probably left Colombury and reached home. It also made sense of the fact that, while the Jaguar was not there, the motorbike was in the locked garage, a fact he had considered to be in Oliver Vail's favour. He had not been able to picture Vail, having killed his mother and decided to bolt, locking the garage door behind him after he had taken the car. But Katie Sorel had unwittingly produced a valid explanation.

"Mrs Sorel, what sort of mood was Mr Vail in yesterday afternoon?"

"Mood?" Katie was disconcerted.

"Yes. For instance, was he annoyed that your former husband had been visiting you, or didn't you tell him?"

"Yes, I told him — but he didn't mind. Oliver wasn't jealous, if that's what you mean. He knew — knows — I love him and want to marry him. Tom won't like it, but he can't prevent it. I'm legally divorced. There's no problem there. I only wish — " Katie stopped, obviously remembering that the problem posed by Mrs Vail no longer existed.

She fidgeted in her seat and looked at her watch. "Chief Inspector, I must go. I had to ask a neighbour to look after Joy. I try not to leave her at her gran's when Tom's at home. Old Mrs Sorel's a dear and very fond of Joy, but she's over seventy and Tom can be — difficult when he likes. So please, I must go. It'll take me half an hour to walk back to Colombury."

"Of course you must go, Mrs Sorel," said Tansey sympathetically. "I may want a formal statement from you, but there's no hurry. It can wait. Meanwhile, there's no need for you to walk. I hadn't realized how you had come here. Sergeant Abbot will drive you home. He can drop me off at the vicarage on the way and pick me up there later."

"Thank you, Chief Inspector. That's very kind of you." Katie managed to smile. "And — and you will let me know when you find out what's happened to Oliver, won't you? Or if you hear anything of him? You can understand how anxious I am."

"Yes. I appreciate that," said Tansey, but he made no promise to keep her informed of the progress of the investigation.

"I do hope you'll discover who did it soon," she continued. "I realize it looks bad for Oliver that his mother's been found dead and he seems to have disappeared, but there must be some explanation. He would never have hurt her. I assure you. Never."

Tansey remained silent. He had nearly

said that Oliver Vail was a lucky man to have someone who had so much faith in him, but he realized in time that the remark would sound at best unkind and at worst condemnatory, and had bitten it back. But five minutes later, as he walked up the path to the vicarage, having said goodbye to Katie Sorel, he caught himself wondering how far Katie's devotion to Oliver would stretch.

If Oliver Vail had killed his mother — and Tansey was far from accepting that this was the case — and had gone on the run, he would probably soon be in difficulties. He was not a criminal, in the sense that he was not a member of the criminal fraternity. Probably his worst offence to date was to be booked for parking on a yellow line. He was a quiet young man who worked in a bank, an only child, living with a domineering mother, or that was the impression that Tansey had received. Not, Tansey was well aware, that this would have prevented Oliver having a sudden brainstorm and killing his mother, but his action would not have been premeditated and therefore it was unlikely that he had made any detailed plans to disappear and escape the consequences.

So, if the police didn't find him first, what would he do? Tansey, judging from experience, believed that Oliver had three choices. Either, in a few days when his money ran out — and Tansey remembered Mrs Vail's missing jewellery — he would give himself up. Or in desperation he would drive the Jaguar over a cliff. Or he would appeal to someone for help, and that someone was most likely to be Mrs Katie Sorel. It would be necessary, he decided, to keep a watch on her.

★ ★ ★

"Hi! Detective Tansey!"

Tansey started. He had been so deep in thought that he had forgotten to go on walking. He was standing on the vicarage path, next to a large bush with yellow flowers that he couldn't name. The voice had come from behind the bush. Now a small girl, ten or twelve years of age, appeared. She was wearing a bright red shirt and khaki shorts that looked too big for her, as if she was expected to grow to fit them.

"You are Detective Tansey," she said, as if wanting confirmation.

"Yes, I'm Tansey."

"How do you do?" She held out a grubby hand. "I'm Janice Moore, the vicar's youngest."

"How do you do?" Solemnly Tansey bent over and shook hands with her. "Oughtn't you to be in school, Miss Moore?" he said. "It's not holidays yet, is it?"

The little girl stared at him. "Miss Moore," she said. "I like that. No, I shouldn't be at school. I'm recovering from chicken-pox."

"I see. Well, I've come to talk to your father."

"And to Meg Denham, who found the Widow's body. I know. That's why I was waiting for you."

"You were? Why?"

"I have some information. I thought you'd like it. The police are always asking for information, aren't they? On the telly and the radio, I mean."

"Yes, we're always grateful for information," Tansey agreed.

"Good. I thought you would be. Well, this is it." Her voice became businesslike. "I don't believe Oliver Vail killed his mother!" she said triumphantly. "I can't prove it, but I do have some circum — circumstantial evidence."

"You do?" Tansey stared at the small girl, ready to believe anything of her at this stage. "That's splendid! What is it?"

"Yesterday evening I was in the woods behind the Vails' house. To be honest I was spying on Alan — that's my eldest brother. I thought he might have had a tryst there with Elaine Pulman. He's very keen on her. And she does take men into the woods," the small girl added with a worldly-wise expression. "But I was wrong. As a matter of fact, I discovered later he was in his room studying. Anyway, it was a few minutes after seven and I have to be home for supper, so I decided to take the short cut through the Vails' property. I saw Oliver dash out of the house. Then I heard a car door slam and a car driving off fast, as if the driver was in a temper. It's my belief that he had a row with his mother and left. Of course he could have come back later, but it seems to me unlikely that he slept on it and then killed her the next morning. What do you think?"

"It's an interesting theory," Tansey said accepting that Janice didn't know the full facts and was assuming that Mrs Vail had been killed that morning. "Was he carrying a bag?"

"Not that I saw."

"Did you see or hear anyone else?"

"I didn't see him, but I think Bert Bilson was somewhere around because I heard a couple of shots a bit earlier and guessed he was after rabbits, though early morning's a better time for rabbiting. Oh, and I saw Miss Gore's lodger — not long after six-thirty that was. He was in a hurry too, almost running out of the woods."

"Janice!" Alan Moore had come out of the house. "Chief Inspector, I hope she's not been bothering you."

"Not at all," said Tansey. "On the contrary, Miss Moore has been most helpful. Thank you." He gave Janice a small bow, and received a conspiratorial grin in return.

"Incidentally, I'm Alan Moore," Alan said. "Do come along in, Chief Inspector." And, as he ushered Tansey into the hall, he added, "I'm afraid I must tell you it's best not to pay too much attention to Jan's stories."

"Why?" asked Tansey. "Does she tell lies?"

"Not direct lies, no, but she puts her own interpretations on the facts. For instance, if she sees two people having an animated conversation she might say they looked as if they were quarrelling or alternatively as if they were arranging an assignation. Mind you," Alan laughed, "sometimes she's right. She's pretty sophisticated for her age, as I'm sure you've gathered."

"Indeed," said Chief Inspector Tansey truthfully. "How very interesting." He was thinking of what Janice had been telling him.

6

"CHIEF INSPECTOR TANSEY," Alan Moore announced, waving Tansey into a large kitchen where two women, each wearing similar floral aprons, were sitting at a well-scrubbed kitchen table, drinking coffee. My mother's the grey-haired one. The other lady is Mrs Denham." He grinned at them.

Unabashed by this introduction Grace Moore said, "Coffee, Chief Inspector? Instant, needless to say. I never have time to do things elegantly. I make good resolutions about getting organized, but in this busy household they remain resolutions and the Moores remain in disarray."

"That's not true, sir," Meg Denham said. "It's a wonderful household, a wonderful family. If all the people I worked for were like the Moores — "

Mrs Moore got up to make Tansey his coffee and he sat down opposite

Meg. By now she had almost completely recovered from the horrifying experience of finding Mrs Vail's body, though she didn't want to think about it. However, she did her best to brace herself for the police officer's inevitable questions. The first one surprised her.

"Did you like working for the Vails, Mrs Denham?" Tansey asked.

"Not much," Meg replied honestly. "Mrs Vail was — fussy and rather difficult. Mr Oliver was all right, but I didn't see him often. I don't get to the house until eight-thirty, and by that time he's usually gone to work."

"What about their breakfasts?"

"They had them earlier before I came. It was always cleared up and everything was carefully arranged in the dishwasher. They ran it once a day after their evening meal."

"Organized," Grace Moore murmured, setting a cup of coffee before Tansey and offering him a plate of biscuits.

A thought seemed to strike Meg Denham. She said, "I don't know if it's important, but of course I didn't look in the dishwasher, so I didn't know that there was anything out of the ordinary this morning." She paused, and when Tansey didn't comment, went on, "I changed my shoes and put on my apron and went to do the sitting-room. Mrs Vail didn't like me to waste time and I expected her to come downstairs any minute."

"As she wasn't down, how did you get into the house?"

"Let myself in as usual. I have a key to the back door."

"It was locked when you arrived?"

"Yes." Meg spoke without hesitation. Nevertheless, the next second her expression changed, and Tansey was alerted. "Are you sure of that, Mrs Denham? Could you swear to it?"

"No-o, sir." Meg was an honest woman. "It always is locked so I suppose it was today, but I couldn't swear to it. I — I was thinking of something else." To her annoyance she felt herself flush as she remembered her husband's tie. "One of my children had been sick during the night."

Tansey left the question of the back door. "Then you didn't notice anything unusual until you went into the sitting-room?"

"I didn't go in. The door was ajar. I remember that clearly because my hands were full, and I only had to push it for it to open and I saw — I saw — Oh God!" Meg turned to Grace Moore. "Mrs Moore, it was dreadful, as I told you! I know I didn't like the Widow, but — but — "

"There, there, Meg," said Grace Moore as if she were speaking to a frightened child. "You've nothing to worry about. You did the right thing and went to get someone who could cope."

"Yes, exactly what did you do next?" Tansey asked.

"I'm not sure. I fled. I couldn't stay in the house, not even to phone, not with — with her lying on the floor there. I got on my bicycle to come to the vicar, but I met him outside the Ploughman's. I fell off my bike, and I told him and the Corbets what I'd seen. Alan Moore and Elaine Pulman were there, and it was they who brought me here for Mrs Moore to look after me."

"The whole thing was very sensible of

you," said Grace Moore.

"And that's all I can tell you, sir," Meg said to Tansey.

"Fine, Mrs Denham. But I do have a couple more questions. Did Mrs Vail pay you by cheque or by cash?"

Meg Denham frowned. "By cash. She always had it ready."

"So she kept money in the house, and she also had some jewellery which seems to be missing. Can you or Mrs Moore describe any of it?"

"Are you thinking she might have interrupted a thief?" Grace Moore asked.

"It's a possibility."

"But why kill her? Why not just run?" Grace Moore wondered aloud. "I suppose he might have lost his head, especially if he was a local and she recognized him. She wasn't the kind of woman to show mercy."

As Grace Moore answered her own question, Tansey saw a look of horror cross Meg Denham's face. He wondered if a possible, or even a probable, culprit had occurred to her, but he didn't pursue the point.

"It's likely that special items will be

described in Mrs Vail's insurance policy," he said, "but if either of you could call to mind some easily identifiable piece that she often wore, we would be able to put a trace out for it at once."

"She didn't wear much jewellery." Surprisingly it was Meg who responded quickly. "Brooches mostly. She had a lot of black stuff — jet, isn't it? — but not valuable." She shrugged, dismissing the subject as unimportant, and again unwittingly arousing Tansey's interest.

Grace Moore had been thinking. "No, Mrs Vail didn't wear much jewellery," she said, supporting Meg. "But she had at least one beautiful diamond brooch — two hearts intertwined. I would guess it was Victorian. And she had a diamond and sapphire ring. I can't recall anything else in particular, but then I only saw her in church on Sundays. She didn't entertain or accept invitations, as far as I know."

"It must have been a dull life for her son."

"Yes, though of course he had his job and friends of his own, but I don't think they visited him at his home very often.

A pity, because he's a nice young man, hard-working and a good son."

Grace Moore looked Tansey in the eye, challenging him to contradict her. But he merely smiled, thanked her and Meg for answering his questions, and asked if it would be convenient for him to speak to the vicar. Grace said he was expected, and suggested that Meg should show him the way to the vicar's study.

★ ★ ★

In the event they met the Reverend Basil Moore in the hall. He was showing out a small bandy-legged man, who gave Tansey a quick and furtive glance before offering the vicar a farewell salute and hurrying past.

"Thanks, Meg," Moore said. "Come along, Chief Inspector. I was expecting you."

He showed Tansey into a large, book-lined, rather shabby room, motioned him to a comfortable armchair, then sat himself down behind a desk that was heaped with books and papers. "Being a parson in a living like this means being a social worker, a barrack-room lawyer and an expert on almost everything. It's like running a local Citizens' Advice Bureau. It's certainly not a sinecure these days — if it ever was."

Tansey laughed. "I'm sure it isn't, and I'm sorry to take up some of your precious time, but unfortunately it's necessary."

"Of course it is, and I don't begrudge the time, Chief Inspector. I assure you I'll help in any way I can. After all, Mrs Vail was one of my parishioners, and so is Oliver. They are — were — both regular churchgoers. But, that apart, it was a shocking, appalling crime, and until the culprit is caught there's going to be a great deal of gossip and recrimination in what is normally a pretty friendly place — and that sort of thing we don't want. I've already come across some of it in the few hours since Mrs Vail was found. Now, having made my position clear, what can I tell you?"

"Would you give me your candid opinion of Mrs Vail and Oliver Vail? I gather Mrs Vail was not popular, but was the antagonism she seems to have aroused due only to the fact that she preferred to live a rather solitary life?"

Basil Moore sighed. "This is going to sound a bit uncharitable, but I regret to say it was largely justified on other grounds. She was undoubtedly a mean woman. For instance, Meg came to work for her one day with the start of a bad cold, and Mrs Vail sent her home after an hour, saying Meg was scattering germs around and she didn't intend to be infected by them. Fair enough, I suppose, but she didn't pay Meg, who has five children and an unemployed husband — not even for that hour. Indeed, Lydia Vail exacted her pounds of flesh from everyone who worked for her and from some who didn't — including Oliver."

Tansey raised his eyebrows and the vicar went on. "Oliver was — what? — seventeen plus when his father died. He told me once that he would have liked to stay at school and go to university, but he hadn't been able to because he couldn't leave his mother. Ten years later and he still wasn't able to leave her, though she was in good health and active. He should have married Katie Sorel long ago, but Mrs Vail didn't approve, and she completely dominated her son. He did what she allowed, but nothing else."

"You've not made him sound a strong character," Tansey said. "In your opinion, Vicar, would Oliver have been capable of killing his mother."

The vicar hesitated. "Not as she was killed, no, Chief Inspector. I can imagine him causing her death deliberately if she were in terrible pain — a so-called mercy killing. He doesn't lack moral courage. But not that frenzied battering. I saw him angry on one occasion when a man was beating a horse, so angry that he was shaking, but he was fully in control of his temper."

"Thank you. I value your judgement," Tansey said slowly.

"But you don't agree with it? I find it hard to believe that things are looking bad for Oliver, but they are, aren't they?"

"Not good, but I try to keep an open mind and there are various contradictions in the evidence — a situation which, I must admit, isn't unusual."

"I can understand that." Basil Moore

was sympathetic. "The number of untruths I've been told in my time as an army padre by perfectly innocent people who had no idea they were lying! It's one of the reasons I would hate to take part in one of those awful identification parades and pick out the guilty man, even if I had witnessed the crime being committed."

Basil Moore smiled at Tansey, and regarded his cluttered desk. It was a clear signal that he had no more to tell the Chief Inspector, and wanted to get on with his own work. Tansey ignored it. He wasn't finished with the vicar.

"Earlier you described Mrs Vail's death as a 'frenzied battering', and therefore you were inclined to exonerate Oliver on the grounds that it would have been completely out of character," Tansey said casually. "When you made that remark did you think of someone in the neighbourhood who does have a violent temper? It would have been natural if you had."

Basil Moore's smile was wry. "How perceptive of you, Chief Inspector. You're backing me into a corner. Yes, I must admit I did — think of someone, I mean.

And if I don't tell you someone else will. Vic Rowe, who lives in Little Chipping with his brother and sister-in-law next to Overton's garage — he has a reputation for violence."

"The gardener, who worked for Mrs Vail, among others?"

"Ah, you've heard of him. Yes. Mostly he's a quiet man, but your own records will show he's been in trouble with the police in Colombury a few times, usually after he's been drinking. However, I've absolutely no reason to believe he would have attacked Mrs Vail."

Before Tansey could answer they heard the front doorbell ring. "That'll probably be my sergeant," said the Chief Inspector.

"Do you want him brought in to us?"

Tansey hesitated. "Not particularly," he said. "If someone could ask him to wait in the car."

"Wait in the car! Nonsense. My wife will look after him," said Moore. "Just a moment." He went to the door and there was a murmur of voices.

When he returned, Tansey, slightly annoyed by the interruption, continued,

"I understand what you mean about Rowe." He nodded his appreciation of what the vicar had said, and also not said. "Now, what about Bert Bilson?"

"Bert Bilson?" The change of subject had startled the vicar. "What has Bert — ? Ah, someone's told you about the dead cat, I suppose. I might have known that story would be resurrected now. Of course it was a stupid thing to do, and unkind. But it may not have been Bert. He always denied it. Some of the village children could have done it — one of Meg's boys perhaps — as a lark."

"But Bert Bilson had a special reason for disliking Mrs Vail, didn't he? Wasn't she going to evict him from his cottage?"

Basil Moore's sigh was one of exasperation rather than resignation. "Chief Inspector, you've been in Little Chipping only a few hours, and you seem to have picked up all the local gossip."

"It's my job, sir. I'm trying to find the person who killed an elderly woman in a particularly brutal fashion."

"Yes. I'm sorry, Chief Inspector," Basil Moore apologized. "You're quite right. But you can scarcely believe Bert was responsible for Mrs Vail's death, not now you've seen him."

"Seen him?" Tansey frowned. "You mean that was Bert Bilson — that weasel-faced little man you were showing out when I met you in the hall?"

"Yes. That was Bert. I can hardly say he's one of my flock, but he uses me as an advice bureau. Today he wanted to know what happens to the wretched cottage since Mrs Vail's dead."

"He didn't waste much time, did he?"

"It's the only home he's got, and at least he wasn't hypocritical about her death. He said he'd rather owe rent to Mr Oliver than to — to Mrs Vail, only he expressed himself somewhat more strongly when he named her."

Tansey wasn't sure that the vicar's championship was altogether in Bert Bilson's favour. Nor was he sure that Bert, had he been hard-pressed, would have been incapable of overpowering Lydia Vail. On the other hand, if he were innocent of her death and full of hope that Oliver would generously forget his rent arrears and bestow the cottage on him, he might be in for a bitter disappointment. Even though — as far as he knew — her will left it to him, Oliver would inherit nothing from his mother if he were proved guilty of her murder; such was English law.

"If you're going to advise Bert Bilson about his rental rights in these circumstances, you'll need to consult Mrs Vail's solicitor. I'll let you know who he is."

"Thanks. I'd be grateful if you would. And now, Chief Inspector, I hope you'll excuse me. I must have something to eat, then change and drive over to Chipping-on-the-Water. I've a wedding at two o'clock." He grinned ruefully. "At least it should be a cheerful event."

Tansey stood up at once. "I must go too. My sergeant will be waiting, and he likes his meals. Thank you for your help, Vicar. I'll be in touch later for a proper statement."

7

GRACE MOORE had done her best for Sergeant Abbot. She had taken him into the vicarage kitchen and produced coffee, a buttered scone and two biscuits. But this had not really been enough to satisfy his growing hunger. Breakfast, with his wife away visiting her mother, had been early and uncooked.

He remembered he had a chocolate bar in the car, and, after thanking Mrs Moore, had said he should perhaps wait in the car to monitor the car phone and because the Chief Inspector should soon be emerging. Grace demurred slightly, but he insisted and now he was sitting in the driver's seat with the windows rolled down, allowing a cool breeze to circulate around him. As he slowly ate his chocolate bar, he thought what a pleasant place Little Chipping was. He wouldn't mind retiring to a village like this someday, though perhaps to one with more character.

He found Kidlington much too busy and noisy, and even Colombury, the small market town where he had spent his boyhood, was growing too big for his liking and had lost much of its charm. He had suggested to his parents that they should move from there, but they refused even to consider the idea.

"Having your lunch, Sergeant Abbot?" Tansey interrupted his musings.

"No, sir, my elevenses — if you can call them that."

Abbot, who had not heard Tansey until he was beside the car, hastily finished his chocolate bar and leaned across to open the door for the Chief Inspector. He hoped Tansey's crack about lunch had been a joke.

"Where to, sir? The Ploughman's?" he asked hopefully.

"No, I don't think so, since we can't turn ourselves into flies on the wall. The pub will be buzzing with stories about the murder and we might pick up some useful points, but more probably everyone will shut up like clams the moment we appear. We'd be an embarrassment to the Corbets."

"Yes, I suppose we would," Abbot agreed mournfully.

Tansey hid his amusement. "We'll go to Colombury and try the Windrush Arms. I'm afraid we'll be too late for the dining-room, but there should be plenty of food at the bar."

"Right." Feeling more cheerful, Abbot started the car. "There was a phone call from Inspector Whitelaw while I was waiting for you, sir. Mrs Vail's body has been removed and is on its way to the mortuary in Oxford. This permitted a search of the floor underneath and a bullet was found in the carpet where her head had been lying. I got the impression he thought there was something odd about this, but I could be wrong."

As Abbot slowed to pass a couple on a tandem bike who, backs bent, seemed to be intent on breaking a speed record of some kind, Tansey said, "And I trust the bullet is on its way to the lab, accompanied by the rifle. Incidentally, has any other weapon been found?"

"No, sir. Inspector Whitelaw believes it's safe to presume that the one beside

Mrs Vail belonged to her and killed her, but we'll know for sure as soon as they do comparison testing on the rifle and the *two* bullets."

"Two bullets?" To Abbot's disappointment Tansey showed only mild surprise. "Where was the second one?"

"In the wall opposite the sitting-room door. The chances are that it was actually fired first when Mrs Vail challenged her assailant. He then seized the rifle from her. They struggled and when he had overcome her, he shot her. At any rate, that's how Inspector Whitelaw sees the scenario."

"And how does Sergeant Abbot see it?"

"It fits, sir, assuming that Mrs Vail surprised a thief, but not so well if it was Oliver. I really can't imagine her shooting at him, unless — "

"Go on," Tansey encouraged.

"Well, I was wondering if perhaps we'd got it the wrong way round, as it were, sir. Supposing Oliver came home and told his ma he was fed up, he'd had enough, he was going to marry Katie Sorel, whatever she said. The old — er — lady realized that this time he meant it. She fetched her rifle and said, 'Over my dead body' or words to that effect. She intended to kill him and then herself, but she missed him. He struggled with her, half killed her and decided to finish her off. Then, overcome by remorse, he fled."

Tansey laughed aloud. He knew he shouldn't. The last thing he wanted was to hurt Bill Abbot's feelings. But he couldn't help it. "I'm sorry, Bill, truly sorry," he said, and managed to suppress another guffaw. "But your vivid representation of what might have happened reminded me of one of those old silent movies they show on television sometimes, the sort that has a piano accompaniment. But, of course, you could be right," he added generously.

Abbot grunted, half mollified by the apology. "It may not be as stupid as it sounds," he said. "When I was driving Katie Sorel back to Colombury she let her hair down a bit. She admitted that Mrs Vail was an old bitch who had prevented Oliver from marrying her, and she said that she had got fed up with the situation. Oliver was a good, kind man, but he wouldn't stand up to his mother. She'd told him that he had to, that he must choose between them, because she refused to go on as they were any longer. Either they arranged to get married in the next three months, or she would stop seeing him."

"An ultimatum, in fact? Did she mean it?"

"I don't know. She says she convinced him, and he promised to speak to his mother and fix a date for the wedding, whatever objections Mrs Vail might have."

"When did all this take place? Yesterday afternoon?"

"Yes, or early evening. When he'd left the bank and called on Mrs Sorel before he went to collect the car from Field's — the Windrush Garage."

"Oh dear! Oh dear!" Tansey said. "That certainly makes your theory more plausible."

★ ★ ★

The Windrush Arms was a small country hotel. Colombury was a good centre for the Cotswolds and in the summer the Windrush had a steady flow of tourists occupying its rooms. The dining-room also did an excellent trade, especially on market days when farmers and growers from the surrounding countryside swelled the number of regulars from the neighbouring shops and businesses. But the heart of the place was its bar.

Always crowded at lunch-time, when Tansey and Abbot arrived the mob was beginning to thin out a little as people started to return to work. Nevertheless, they were lucky to find a table in a comparatively private corner. With pints of bitter and a plate heaped with sandwiches full of thick juicy ham in front of them, plus a few sausages, they settled down to their meal.

When the edge had been taken off his appetite, Abbot said, "Could you tell me how you got on at the vicarage, sir?"

"Sure, if you don't mind my speaking with my mouth full." Tansey bit into a sandwich, thankful that however much he ate he never put on weight. "My first meeting was with Miss Moore, aged about ten, who accosted me as I arrived."

He went on to recount what Janice had told him, and Abbot listened with interest. "The girl was right about one thing, sir," he said. "Bert Bilson was rabbiting yesterday evening."

Tansey raised his eyebrows. "How do you know that?"

"Because — " Abbot was slightly abashed. "While you were talking to the vicar, sir, I was in the kitchen with Mrs Moore and saw a rabbit. She said Bert Bilson had brought it in, that he often did, that he was an old rogue, but had only his pension to live on and she was glad to buy rabbits from him occasionally."

Tansey, who had been raising his tankard to his mouth, put it down again and regarded Abbot seriously. "We shall have to go and talk to this man and to Janice again. Janice said she heard shots. She assumed they were Bilson's, and so they may have been. But what about the two shots that we now know were fired inside the Vails' house? Were they those she heard, or were they really Bilson's? And we must try and check on the times. Janice had to be home by seven-thirty. I guess she's fairly dependable, and let's hope, though I wouldn't count on it, that Bilson had an equally important date, or at least a reliable watch."

"You don't think — " Abbot began. "Bert Bilson could be said to have a motive for wishing Mrs Vail dead. She may have been within her rights wanting to turn him out of her cottage, but it was an unpleasant thing to do. No one would have rented the place, and Bilson would have been homeless."

"Who knows?" said Tansey. "The one thing I'm sure of at this point is that Mrs Vail did not have a reputation for charity."

Tansey briefed Abbot on his own meetings with Mrs Moore and Mrs Denham and then with the vicar. Then they continued to discuss the case, the need to check on Vic Rowe's police record, what Oliver Vail might do next, the possibility that the killer was a professional thief, the mystery of why he had washed in both the downstairs cloakroom and the upstairs bathroom.

Finally, Abbot got up to fetch more beer and sandwiches. By now there were noticeably fewer people in the bar, but one or two newcomers were still arriving.

A large ginger-haired man with the ruddy face of an outdoor worker came in. He strode to the bar, banged on it and shouted for his usual. Then he slapped a man sitting beside him on the back, causing him to spill his drink.

"Hi there, Tom Sorel!" he said. "Long time no see. When did you return to this neck of the woods, mate?" The ginger man had a large booming voice that carried throughout the pub.

The man addressed swung round on his bar stool as if to protest, but, seeing who it was, greeted the newcomer with pleasure. "Hi-yer, Ken! I got home the day before yesterday."

"Home? You mean your ma's? Was she glad to see the wandering boy?"

"Of course. She always is, bless her. After all, I'm her only. Too bad I followed my old dad's profession and became a merchant seaman."

The man called Ken roared with laughter. "Like father, like son, eh, mate?" he said. "You been to see that bitch of a wife of yours yet?"

"I been to see my poor kid. I have legal rights."

"*Your* poor kid! That's what she told you, but you can't trust these women."

Tom Sorel went an unhealthy red and said something in a low voice that neither Tansey nor Abbot could hear. They were watching the encounter and straining to overhear the conversation between the two men, intrigued by this chance meeting with Katie's ex-husband. He was a big, strong man, fair-haired, blue-eyed and, except for a nasty slash across his forehead, extremely good looking — more like a film star, Abbot thought, than a seaman. Tansey, who was more observant than his sergeant, also wondered when Sorel had last been at sea; if so, he certainly hadn't been in the tropics recently, for his skin was pale.

"Sorry, mate! Sorry!" Ken was saying. "No offence, mate. Here, let me buy you a drink. What'll you have? Christ! Scotch! At today's prices. Your ship *must* have come in, mate."

"There's nothing to spend your money on during a long voyage, so you save your pay whether you mean to or not," Sorel said carelessly. "But if it's your shout, Ken, I'll have a beer chaser. What are you up to these days, still lorry-driving?"

As Ken started a lengthy monologue on the advantages and disadvantages of long-distance truck driving — he had just returned from a trip across Europe to the Middle East, and was taking a few days' leave before setting off again — a waitress came to the detectives' table to collect their empties.

"Who's that chap by the bar over there?" Tansey asked her casually, nodding in the direction of Sorel and his companion.

"You mean with the Smasher?" she said.

"The Smasher?"

"The good-looking guy — Tom Sorel. We call him the Smasher. The other man is Ken Coster. They were at school here together with my brother, which is how I know, even though they're not often in Colombury these days."

"Thanks," Tansey said. "I thought it was someone I once knew, but it isn't."

★ ★ ★

Shortly afterwards time was called and the bar emptied. Tansey and Abbot strolled along the High Street in the sunshine.

"That," said Tansey with satisfaction, "was an excellent meal and time well spent. Let's hope it was a good omen."

8

FROM the Windrush Arms to the Windrush Garage on the outskirts of Colombury is a fifteen-minute walk after lunch in summer when the pavements are crowded with tourists, shoppers, prams, children and locals returning to their jobs. But for once Chief Inspector Tansey didn't resent the delays, not even when Abbot was stopped by an old friend who was determined to chat. He was happy to have some spare time to ruminate on the case.

Or he should have been happy. It was only a few hours since the body had been discovered. Inspector Whitelaw had organized the scene of crime team with his usual efficiency. The doctors, Band and Ghent, police surgeon and pathologist, had been and gone. The remains of Lydia Vail would by now have reached the mortuary and Forensic were being unusually cooperative, promising quick reports. Inquiries were going well.

There were some anomalies, some things which didn't make sense, but there always were, in any case, however simple it might seem at the outset. So why did he have this feeling of unease, this sense of urgency, as if — as if — ? He didn't know what, but he wished he did, for somehow he sensed that the point was of considerable importance.

"Here we are, sir. Field's garage." Abbot broke into his thoughts. "Sorry about meeting that chap. He works on the *Courier*, and incidentally he told me that someone had phoned in with the news of Mrs Vail's murder, and one of their reporters was on his way to Little Chipping."

Tansey grunted. He knew that by 'someone' Abbot meant Sergeant Donaldson, who had been suspected before now of tipping off the press, but he didn't want to encourage Abbot's dislike of Donaldson, which seemed due to little except personal antipathy. Besides, it didn't matter; the media would soon be at Little Chipping in force, and he would be compelled to hold a press conference.

"Can I help you, gentlemen?" A small

grey-haired man in a business suit, seeing them standing on the garage forecourt, had come out of the building. "Why, hello, Bill," he continued. "I didn't recognize you at first."

"'Afternoon, Mr Field. This is Detective Chief Inspector Tansey from our headquarters at Kidlington. I'm afraid we're here on police business."

"Chief Inspector." He nodded at Tansey. "Come along in. If it's a question of records, I've a clear conscience."

He led the way into a well-furnished office which confirmed the general impression provided by the neatly-uniformed mechanics, the spotless forecourt and the fresh paintwork, that this was an efficient and prosperous establishment, and invited them to sit down.

"Coffee?" he asked.

They refused, saying they had just finished lunch. Then Tansey launched into the subject of their visit.

"We're making inquiries about a Jaguar which you sold to Mrs Lydia Vail of Little Chipping at the end of last year — about six months ago," he said.

Field's eyes widened. "Yes, that's right. What's happened? Has she had an accident? It must be important for a Chief Inspector to be interested."

Tansey ignored Field's question. "The car was registered, and all the insurance papers and so on were made out in her name, I assume?"

"Yes, but it's also insured for another person to drive, and her son, Oliver Vail, does drive it sometimes. But what — "

"Such as yesterday. He brought it into your garage yesterday morning. Is that correct?"

"Yes. That's correct, and it's not the first time it's been brought in." Field sighed. "Frankly, I was pleased to sell Mrs Vail a brand new Jag. Business hasn't been all that good recently. But I've almost regretted it since. She's always complaining that there's something wrong with the car. The last thing was supposed to be a squeaky steering-wheel, but we couldn't trace it, and it took a couple of hours of a mechanic's time, which doesn't come cheap — and which I have to pay for. I regret to say I was a bit short with poor Oliver when he collected it."

"When was that?"

"Yesterday evening, between five-thirty and six."

"Can you be more precise, Mr Field?"

"Not really. It was after five-thirty and before six because we shut at six. The pumps are self-service, so we don't have to worry about them after hours." Field paused and frowned. "I would say it was probably about a quarter to the hour. He was here perhaps five minutes, not more, and then he drove off. Chief Inspector, why all these questions?"

"Mr Field, it's already public knowledge. Mrs Vail has been killed."

"In the car?"

"No. At her house. We are treating the matter as a murder inquiry."

"Good Heavens! In Little Chipping. But why these questions about the Jag and Oliver? You surely can't think — Oliver's the mildest of fellows."

"Mr Field, the investigation has just commenced. We're nowhere near accusing anyone or making an arrest. However, we do know that Mrs Vail died yesterday evening, and we're trying to narrow down the time during which her death may have occurred."

"And you've been a great help, Mr Field," Abbot said quickly, realizing from the Chief Inspector's clipped tone that the interview was at an end, and guessing that Tansey didn't wish to answer any more questions about Oliver and the Jaguar.

"Yes, indeed," Tansey said, pushing back his chair and standing up. "You've confirmed what we've already been told. Many thanks, Mr Field."

Field smiled at them. He was an intelligent man, accustomed to dealing with people, and though he was full of curiosity he knew that it was not going to be satisfied. "Always glad to help the police," he said, standing and preparing to see them out. "I can produce all the records of the sale of the Jag and the details of the car whenever you want. I can't honestly say I liked Mrs Vail much, but there's too much violence around these days, much too much. I hope you get whoever did it, and soon."

★ ★ ★

The next stop for Tansey and Abbot was the bank where Oliver Vail had been a clerk for the last ten years. They identified themselves to the manager's secretary, and were asked to wait a few minutes.

It was not long before Mr Clement, the manager, appeared, showing out a man who was obviously a client.

"Sorry about making you wait," he said, "you should have phoned first."

"I know," said Tansey, "but we were passing, and we thought we'd take a chance."

Unlike Mr Field, Clement had been told early that morning that Mrs Vail was dead and sometime later had learnt that she had been brutally murdered. The news had appalled him. He didn't care about Mrs Vail. He didn't know her. She wasn't a customer. But Oliver Vail worked in his bank and Oliver seemed to have disappeared.

David Clement was a kind and thoughtful man, and he had no wish to cast suspicion on Oliver — suspicion which might prove to be totally unjustified; he knew what gossip was like in a small town. Nevertheless, his duty to the bank had to come first.

He had chosen his most trusted assistant, explained the situation to her, and asked her to check on all the accounts to which Oliver Vail had access. This was not an easy task, as he explained to Tansey and Abbot. Nothing untowards had been found, though there was one point he must bring to the attention of the police, and he had decided that unless they could give him some reassurances concerning Oliver he must report the matter to Oxford and thus to the head office in London.

"I regret to say, Mr Clement," Tansey replied, "that I cannot give you any reassurances for we don't know where he is at present, or what might have happened to him. We know that when he left work he went to visit a friend, and then to the Windrush Garage to collect his mother's car. But we don't know what his movements were after six o'clock yesterday evening."

"I may be able to help you there, Chief Inspector," said Clement. "Just after nine-thirty this morning he was at the Midland Bank main branch in Reading."

"Reading? How do you know that?"

"Well, you know the form as well as I do. You can cash a cheque at another branch of the same bank for up to £100 on production of an appropriate card. If you want more than that sum the branch has to phone the account-holding branch, to make sure the money's available. This they did; the call was logged at nine-thirty-eight a.m. The clerk here checked, noted that it almost cleared the account, but gave her OK, with a reference number."

"I understand," Tansey said.

He glanced at Abbot and made a small gesture, his mind teeming with questions. He would begin asking some of them. Then he hoped Abbot would interject his own remarks, and with any luck the bank manager could be persuaded to overcome his scruples and tell them everything they needed to know. But Clement would have to be treated gently.

"Mr Clement, that's a great help," he said, wishing they had had this information sooner. "How much money did Mr Vail draw out in Reading?"

"Three hundred pounds from his current account. It was small at this time of the month, and this withdrawal almost cleared it out, as I said. He's attempted to withdraw nothing since. He would be allowed a small overdraft, though I don't think he's ever asked for one." Clement smiled apologetically. "Of course, you appreciate that this is all in confidence, gentlemen? That's why I don't want to go into exact figures."

"Of course," said Tansey.

Abbot asked, "Mr Clement, was it usual for Mr Vail to have about three hundred in his current account at this time of the month?"

"That would be about its upper limit. It might go down a little below that, but as far as I can tell, he was a careful chap with money."

"But he lived up to his income? Now, you mentioned 'current' account. Did he have savings — in some deposit account, say, Mr Clement?"

"Yes, he has a deposit account — two weeks' notice." Clement sounded reluctant.

"That's why he would have been allowed an overdraft."

"How much?" This was Tansey.

Clement hesitated. Then, "Fifty pounds — now."

"Perhaps you'd explain, Mr Clement. It's probably irrelevant. Half the questions we ask and the answers we get are irrelevant, but sometimes a chance piece of information helps us to make sense of what seemed meaningless, or completes a pattern for us."

Clement hesitated again. "Well, in the circumstances, I'll try to explain. Until five months ago Vail had almost three thousand pounds in his deposit account. He transferred regular sums into it each month from his current account. Then he gave the necessary warning to avoid penalty, and drew out the lot. What's more, when I asked him jokingly if he were planning a trip around the world, he was quite short with me, which was most unusual for him."

"Maybe he was planning to get married," Tansey said.

"I don't know. I just don't understand it. He was a nice young man — is a nice young man." Clement was torn between his previous opinion and liking of Oliver Vail and the obvious evidence against him. "I don't know what to think."

Tansey shifted the subject. Clement was running dry as a source of information. "Did Vail have any particular friends among your staff?" he asked.

"No." Clement shook his head. "This isn't a large branch and we don't have any clubs or societies, but he never came to such social events as we do have — like the Christmas party and the summer picnic. He always made excuses. But that's not to say he wasn't popular. He was helpful and obliging and everyone liked him. I can't believe he would have killed — anyone."

★ ★ ★

"The manager picked up the implications of what we were asking pretty quickly, didn't he, sir?" Abbot said after they had been ushered out of the bank. "It's amazing, isn't it, how no one can believe that an individual they know and like could actually be a murderer?"

126

"It makes them doubt their own judgement," said the Chief Inspector. He had stopped walking, and Abbot was forced to do the same. "Didn't Katie Sorel say she lived just around the corner from the bank?"

"Yes, sir. We've just passed her lane. It's the second cottage on the right."

"OK. I think I'm going to pay her a surprise visit. One of us, will be enough, though — less official. Meanwhile, I want you to find out the name of Mrs Vail's firm of solicitors from Inspector Whitelaw. He'll have all the private papers from her desk. Ask him — no, you do it, Abbot. Make an appointment for me to see the partner who drafted her will tomorrow morning *first thing* if he's within reasonable reach, later if he's a Londoner. Use your common sense. And don't expect any excuses. This is a murder inquiry."

"Yes, sir," said Sergeant Abbot, wondering what he should do if the firm turned out to be located in Glasgow, especially as he had no idea what the Chief Inspector had in mind for the rest of the day. "Anything else?"

"Yes. I promised to let Basil Moore have the solicitor's name, so you can do that."

"Yes, sir."

"And there's something else. Go through Vic Rowe's record here in Colombury with Donaldson; then check with Central Records to see if there's anything elsewhere."

"Very good, sir."

"I shan't be long, Abbot. Wait for me in the car. After this, I must speak to Whitelaw in the Incident Van. Then, barring the unexpected, we'll be going straight back to Headquarters to report and check if anything's come in."

Tansey turned away, not waiting for Abbot's response, and headed for Green Lane, where Katie Sorel lived. He swore softly as a small boy on a skateboard drove into his ankle. He set the boy back on his two legs and, unaware that he was frowning fiercely, was surprised when the child picked up the board and ran off.

It was Abbot's query, "Anything else?" that was worrying Tansey. He was sure at the back of his mind that there was something else — and something that mattered — but for the life of him he couldn't remember what it was, and the question nagged at him. With an effort he put it from him and knocked on Katie Sorel's door.

* * *

The cottages along Green Lane, solid little buildings of Cotswold stone, were copies of each other. All that distinguished them were the colours of their front doors and their curtains. Katie's front door, which like the others gave directly on to the street with no pavement, was painted dark blue. As he waited for her to open it, Tansey guessed that for the inhabitants the picturesqueness of the exteriors didn't compensate for the inconvenience of the interiors.

"Chief Inspector!" Katie had opened the door and was staring at him, wide-eyed. "Oliver? You've found him? Is he — is he all right?" Involuntarily she had seized Tansey's arm.

"As far as we know, yes, he's all right, Mrs Sorel. But we still don't exactly know where he is now, though he was in Reading early this morning."

"Reading?" Katie released Tansey's arm.

"Perhaps I could come in," he said.

"Yes, I'm sorry," she said, taking a step back and repeating, "Reading?"

Shutting the front door behind him, Tansey found himself in a dark, narrow hall. To the left was a flight of stairs, immediately ahead a door which he guessed led to the kitchen, and to the right an open door through which Katie gestured him. He went in, expecting the room to be the conventional front parlour that is usual in such cottages. He was wrong.

Indeed, it was one of the most oddly furnished rooms he had ever seen. It was small, and somehow managed to appear both bare and cluttered at the same time. It contained an armchair, and beside it a table on which was heaped what he took to be a pile of women's magazines and a cheap radio. There was an electric sewing machine and chair — a length of brocade cascaded from it on to the floor — and in the corner two long evening dresses hung on a stand. Katie, it seemed, was a dressmaker.

But while he accepted these facts, Tansey's attention was centred on the other occupant of the room. This was a small girl, seated in a miniature armchair. She had dark hair like her mother's and blue eyes shaded by long dark lashes. She was quite the most beautiful child Tansey had ever seen, except that she lacked any animation. She had paid no attention to his arrival and seemed concentrated on the length of brocade that lay on the floor. She might have been a doll. Indeed, this comparison was strengthened by the way she was dressed. She wore a blue silk frock, with a matching bow in her hair, white socks, silver shoes; she looked as her grandmother might have done, dressed up for some special occasion.

"My daughter, Joy," Katie Sorel said.

"Hello, Joy," Tansey said, smiling at her, but she ignored him completely and he turned to Katie. "It's a lovely day. Oughtn't she to be out playing? Do you have a garden?"

"Joy doesn't play," Katie said. "She's

131

not like other children. She lives in a world of her own, but I think she's happy. She responds to me and she has likes and dislikes. She likes pretty things, materials and flowers and she hates being dirty. And she accepts Oliver."

"But why — "

"No one knows. She was born like that. Autistic, it's called. Sorel — my ex-husband — wanted to put her in a home when we discovered she was different, but I refused, and I've not regretted it. She's mine and I love her."

There was no answer to that, Tansey thought. Katie Sorel was not one of life's lucky beings, an abnormal child, a broken marriage, and now Oliver Vail. He had decided to visit her on impulse. He had some questions to ask her and, vaguely wondering if Oliver kept her in comparative comfort, had wanted to see her at home. Faced with the reality of her situation he felt slightly ashamed. He would ask his questions and go.

Katie forestalled him. "Chief Inspector, you said Oliver was in Reading this morning. How — how do you know?"

He explained and added, "Have you

132

any idea why he should have chosen Reading? Has he ever mentioned friends there?"

"No. I don't think he has any close friends. He's lost touch with the boys he was at school with, and his colleagues at the bank were fairly casual."

"Relations?"

"He's never spoken of any. I'm sure he would have by this time. We're very good friends."

"Did you know that a few months ago he drew out nearly all his savings, amounting to two or three thousand pounds?"

"Yes!"

Well, he'd asked the main question he had come to ask and received his answer. "You did?"

"Yes. He insisted and I couldn't refuse. I would never have taken the money for myself, but if there was any hope for Joy I couldn't deny her, could I? Only there wasn't. We spent three weeks in London, Joy and me. She saw all sorts of specialists and had all sorts of tests. Oliver arranged everything. He was as sad as I was when we learnt she'd never be like other children. He's very fond of her and, as I said, she — she accepts him; I think she even likes him."

Katie's voice broke and for a moment she couldn't continue. Then she said, "Oliver's a good man, Chief Inspector, really good. You must believe that. I know his mother's been killed, and I know he's behaving in a strange fashion, but I'm sure he's innocent and you must prove it, Chief Inspector. You must."

"I'll try, Mrs Sorel," Tansey said but he knew he couldn't do the impossible.

9

BACK in his Kidlington office, Tansey was awaiting Inspector Whitelaw's arrival. When he had spoken to the Incident Van he had suggested that he and Whitelaw should meet at Headquarters and, after a bite of supper in the canteen, consider the progress of the case, which seemed to be becoming increasingly confused, and discuss possibilities and suppositions. He asked Whitelaw to bring with him any important reports he had not seen.

"A policeman's lot!" exclaimed Inspector Whitelaw, sinking into a chair opposite the Chief Inspector at about seven o'clock that evening, and knowing that they had at least a couple of hours work ahead of them. "Why did I ever choose this as a career? I might have gone in for crime. It would have been an easier life."

Tansey grinned, thankful that Inspector Whitelaw was in a good humour. "I know. I'm sorry about this, Maurice, but

I've a press conference at ten tomorrow, and I have to see Mrs Vail's lawyer first. I must get things clear in my head. After we've been to the canteen, I suggest we try to collate the hard evidence we've got so far and try to plan some future course of action."

They were both experienced officers and they had always got on well together. Tansey's use of Whitelaw's first name was a signal that this was a moment to forget rank; this would be an informal meeting which, they hoped, would bring them nearer to their mutual aim — to apprehend the killer of Lydia Vail.

When they returned from the canteen Whitelaw opened his briefcase and arranged his notes on his side of Tansey's desk. "Shall I start?" he said and, when Tansey nodded, commenced, "The body of a woman, later identified as Lydia Olive Vail, widow of Lionel — "

"Skip it," Tansey said. "First of all, let's assume what we both know and dive in and think a bit about suspects. Primarily one can divide them into Oliver Vail, or someone such as Bert Bilson or Vic Rowe, or a complete stranger. The main thing about Oliver is that he's made himself scarce."

"Fair enough," said Inspector Whitelaw. "And there's the question of the rifle which battered her to death. It was hers. The serial number on the weapon corresponds with that on her firearms certificate. And, what's more, the only person likely to know where she kept it is Oliver."

"I gather you've found two rounds, and they were both fired from that rifle?" said Tansey.

"True. Both bullets came from the rifle. Forensic have been quick and helpful for once. They can't be as busy as they pretend. From where the bullets were found and the angles of their trajectories, the first — the one found in the wall opposite the sitting-room door — could well have been fired during a struggle between the victim and her assailant — "

"We know there was a struggle?" asked Tansey.

"Yes. Because Dr Ghent has identified two types of blood in the sitting-room, which means Mrs Vail must have inflicted some damage on her opponent. Incidentally, Ghent would like to do the post-mortem tomorrow afternoon if that's all right with you. He'll expect you at two p.m. unless he hears to the contrary."

"OK." Tansey sighed. He hated post-mortems, but there was no way of avoiding them. "Go on. What about the second bullet?"

"Either she was dead by then, or very near death. She must have been lying on her back and from the trajectory angle it appears that someone stood over her and deliberately shot her in the head."

"There must have been prints on the rifle."

"Several, but all very smeared as if someone had tried to wipe it. I hope for a full report tomorrow."

"Fine. Well, let's think of a possible sequence of events, as far as we can. Mrs Vail was in her bedroom and heard unexplained sounds below. Believing there was an intruder in the house, she collected her rifle — I would imagine she kept it upstairs so that it would be available at night; after all, it is quite an isolated house — and went

138

down to confront him. I haven't got the impression that she was a shy, frightened woman. I think this could have been in character."

"Yes, but why didn't she assume the noise she heard was Oliver coming in?"

"Perhaps he always announced his return. I don't know. Anyway she goes downstairs and confronts whoever it is. They struggle. He seizes the gun and it goes off, to embed the first round in the wall. Then he overpowers her and kills her, making sure with a further shot. Because she had recognized him, and he couldn't risk her surviving long enough to mutter his name, or because he lost control of himself? No, the second theory's not very likely." Tansey answered his own question. "In that case the simplest thing for him to do would have been to go on battering her. Why fire the rifle again?"

"This scenario assumes that the killer was not Oliver," Whitelaw said. "But, after all, it was Oliver who had the means, the opportunity and a motive. In fact, a double motive. According to local gossip supplied by villagers via Sergeant

Donaldson, his mother was preventing him from marrying Katie Sorel, and according to the will that WPC Norton found he inherits everything, though not of course if he's guilty of his mother's murder. What's more, Dick, as you say, he's now bolted, though he's not gone abroad. He left his passport behind."

"Anyhow, it can't have been premeditated or he wouldn't have killed her this way," replied Tansey. "He may have been dominated by his mother, but no one has suggested the man's a fool. I suppose they could have quarrelled over Katie and he could have lost his temper, but what then? Did he go and fetch the rifle? Or had she brought it down, thinking him to be an intruder?"

"No. That is a problem — one of them."

"Is there any hard evidence to support the idea that it was not Oliver?"

"You'd have to scratch for anything really hard. Cash and jewellery missing, but Oliver might have taken them. The more obvious video recorder was left behind, and Mrs Vail's mink coat. Bert Bilson certainly had a motive — his cottage — and we know that Vic Rowe was given to violent rages. He's been in jug twice for assault, I was told, according to Records. But there have been no reports of suspicious strangers — or any strangers, for that matter, in the village. No, Oliver's the obvious suspect."

"Yes," Tansey agreed reluctantly, and thought of Katie Sorel and the beautiful child lost in her dreams. "But it could have been a casual thief, a vagrant living rough or someone, wondering if there was any work going, who just seized a chance. He could have rung the back doorbell, received no answer, and — "

"It's possible," Whitelaw interjected, "there's something wrong with the wiring and it only rings intermittently. He could have tried the door and gone in. But surely the door wouldn't have been left unlocked. They were careful about security. All the doors have got good sound locks with deadlatches and gadgets that can be fixed to need a key or not. I would guess the Vails used the back door rather than the front, because it's closer to the garage."

Tansey said, "Meg Denham, the cleaner, couldn't remember whether it was locked or not when she arrived this morning. Are there any signs of illegal entry elsewhere?"

"Surprisingly, yes. It looks as if someone fairly recently climbed into the house through the window of the utility room, but then again that could have been Oliver, who might have forgotten his key and didn't want to disturb his mother. No, Dick, there's really nothing to support this kind of theory. Everything points to the missing Oliver."

Tansey didn't comment. Instead he changed the subject. "What about times? Has Ghent managed to fix the time of death any more closely yet?"

"Not Ghent, but WPC Norton."

"What?"

She pointed out that the table wasn't laid for the evening meal, so it's a fair surmise that the murder took place before eight-thirty, unless of course the Vails had already eaten and everything had been cleared away. Norton then explored the kitchen. There were breakfast and presumably lunch plates neatly stacked in the dishwasher, but not enough to account for dinner."

"According to Meg Denham, they ran the dishwasher once a day after their evening meal."

"Good. That's confirmation. Would Meg know at what time they usually ate?"

"We could ask." Tansey reached for the telephone.

Meg was sorry, but she couldn't help. She never cooked or prepared meals for the Vails. Mrs Vail gave her a light lunch on Tuesdays and Thursdays, days that Oliver didn't come home at midday, and she always left at four-thirty.

"No luck," said Tansey. "Let's try Katie Sorel."

Katie picked up the receiver after the first ring, as if she were expecting or at least hoping for a call. Tansey at once said there was no news of Oliver. A heavy sigh came down the line, but when he explained why he had phoned, she responded readily.

"Yes. It was absurd really — a sort of ceremony," she said. "They 'dined', as Mrs Vail insisted it should be called, at seven forty-five every evening in the dining-room. Very formal! Oliver had to be home by seven. He and I used to laugh about it, say it gave him time to wash his hands like a good little boy before he and his mama had a drink together. But he did what she wanted, all the same." Katie's voice trailed away sadly.

Tansey thanked her, said goodbye and told Whitelaw what he'd learnt. "I think we're safe to say the murder took place before seven-forty-five, but can we do better than that? The meal wouldn't have got itself. Were there any signs of preparation?"

"Yes. Norton worked out exactly what they were going to have. There was homemade soup in a saucepan, waiting to be heated up. There was a casserole in the oven, but unluckily the cooker was turned to automatic, so the oven would have gone on, cooked the food and turned itself off and is therefore no help to us as regards time. But there was a chocolate pudding in the fridge which, according to my culinary expert, would have been made about two hours before it was expected to be eaten."

"That assumes that Mrs Vail was an expert cook, and was careful about timing." Tansey was sceptical.

"I think that's a safe assumption," Whitelaw said. "Norton tasted all the food and assured me it was excellent. She also pointed out a long shelf of well-thumbed cookery books in the kitchen."

"All right. We have two times. Seven-forty-five when the Vails should have been sitting down to their dinner, and about five-forty-five when Mrs Vail was supposedly making the pudding. I'm not wholly happy about the second time, Maurice. However the two-hour period would be acceptable to Band and Ghent and would fit what the Moore child told me. I must have another serious talk with her. It's beginning to look as if she could turn out to be quite an important witness."

"That's a pity. No one ever trusts children's evidence." Whitelaw smothered a yawn. "Sorry."

"Don't apologize. It's been a hard day for both of us, and tomorrow doesn't promise to be much better." Tansey thought of the press conference and the post-mortem. "Worse, if anything. I suggest we go home now. After all, we've achieved a fair amount today, Maurice, and I really don't think we can do any more. We haven't exactly achieved what we set out to do, I suppose — make a plan and all that. But it'll have to wait. Agreed?"

"Agreed, Dick," said Inspector Whitelaw thankfully. "I don't think there's any more to be done tonight. Let's hope Oliver Vail turns up tomorrow."

"You believe Oliver's guilty, don't you?" Tansey said as they started to collect together their papers in preparation for leaving the office.

Whitelaw shrugged. "He certainly seems to me to be the best bet."

Tansey nodded. He couldn't disagree.

★ ★ ★

Dick Tansey couldn't sleep, tired though he was. He lay on his back, eyes closed and tried not to fidget; he didn't want to wake his wife, Hilary, who was breathing gently and rhythmically in the bed beside him. For a minute or two he relaxed as he thought with love and affection of her and the child she was carrying. Then his brain began to race again as he went over and over the events of the day, the people involved with Lydia Vail's death, the evidence given — and withheld — the possible lies told, the deceptions, the lead that he had missed.

Everything pointed to the good, kind, quiet young man whom everyone liked. Why else had Oliver Vail bolted? Tansey could think of no reason, however far-fetched. And if Oliver wasn't the guilty party, who was? The list of conceivable suspects wasn't long. He had been over it in his mind many times.

But the list could easily grow. Tansey reminded himself that Lydia Vail had not been a popular woman. There would be others whom he had not yet met, others in the neighbourhood, even in Little Chipping, who might have a grudge against the Widow. He must take his own advice, and remember that the case was still young.

Gradually Tansey drifted into sleep,

only to wake a couple of hours later, sweating heavily. He had had an appalling nightmare. He had dreamed that Hilary's child had been born but immediately she had become four or five years old. In the dream, she bore a strong resemblance to WPC Norton, but her name was Joy and, like Joy Sorel, she lived in a world of her own. "It's all your fault, Dick," Hilary had said in his dream. "All your fault. You're looking in the wrong direction."

Tansey forced himself fully awake. He knew it had been a nightmare, easily explicable by the day's events, and he was not a superstitious man, but he sat on the side of the bed for the next fifteen minutes, and wondered about the death of Lydia Vail and in which direction he should be looking.

10

THE residue of the nightmare stayed with Tansey the next day, causing him to be more demanding of himself than was strictly necessary. After a light breakfast he went into Headquarters early, but achieved nothing. There was no news of either Oliver Vail or the Jaguar, and an hour spent studying the file on the Vail case brought no new insight or flash of inspiration.

Resigned, he set off for the offices of Browne, Browne and Waller-Clive in Oxford. It was Mr Waller-Clive who had drawn up Lydia Vail's will that had been found in her desk. Waller-Clive turned out to be a surprisingly young man, and not what Tansey imagined would have been Mrs Vail's choice of lawyer.

"Come in, come in, Chief Inspector," he said cheerfully as his secretary showed Tansey into his office. "I know why you're here. I've read all about it in the local rag. Quite a shock. Horribly gruesome." He waved to a chair. "Sit you down."

"Thank you." Tansey sat. "Did you know Mrs Vail well?"

"Scarcely knew her at all. I doubt if she was here half a dozen times."

"Nevertheless, her death was a shock to you?"

"Yes. She was my very first client. That would be almost ten years ago now. Uncle Willy — William Browne, Senior — passed her on to me. He said making her will was a simple matter and I couldn't go wrong."

Tansey yearned to ask Mr Waller-Clive if he had gone wrong. Instead, he said, "The will must have been made soon after Mrs Vail became a widow and moved to Little Chipping, but she must have had a lawyer before that to deal with her husband's estate, who could and probably would have mentioned your firm to her. Would your records show who that was?"

Waller-Clive was shaking his head. "She told me her husband died intestate, but he had nothing to leave. He had been

150

a sick man for many years, and their total income, inherited from her father, had been hers."

"You remember that — from ten years ago?" Tansey made no attempt to hide his disbelief.

"No. I looked up the file when I heard on the radio that she had been murdered and then someone made an appointment for you to see me. I had made notes at the time." Waller-Clive looked and sounded pleased with himself.

"Then perhaps, if it wasn't another lawyer, you'll tell me who it was who recommended your firm."

"Mrs Vail's bank manager at the Midland main branch here in Oxford, where she had just opened accounts, transferred from the Isle of Wight where she had lived. And that's all I can tell you about her, Chief Inspector, except that she was a fierce lady. Frankly, she scared me."

"To your knowledge, this is her last will?"

Waller-Clive took the copy that Tansey held out to him and compared it with the original on the file in front of him.

"To our knowledge, yes. Very simple, leaving everything to her son, Oliver; if he predeceased her, everything to charity. If a later will turns up, I can assure you it wasn't drawn up by this firm."

"Thank you. That's most helpful. Now, one more question. You said you doubted if you'd met Mrs Vail more than half a dozen times. Exactly how often did you meet her, at what intervals and when was the last?"

Waller-Clive frowned, as if deep thought were required. "Four — no — five times. The last was three weeks ago."

"All concerning the will? Was she planning to change it?"

"No. The first two interviews were concerned with taking her instructions for the will and going over the final text with her before she signed it. You can see for yourself, it was witnessed here in the office and it gives the date. That was ten years ago, as I said. Then four years ago she suddenly phoned and asked for an appointment. I'd forgotten who she was, to be truthful. I had to look her up in our files." Waller-Clive grinned as if sharing a joke with Tansey.

"What did she want then?"

"To add a codicil to her will stating in effect that if her son Oliver Vail married a divorced woman, he could no longer inherit from her. However, we advised her against it, on the grounds that it quite likely wouldn't hold water these days. Oliver would sensibly contest the codicil and a judge could well not uphold it."

"I see," Tansey said and wondered if Oliver Vail had known of this, if perhaps his mother had lied to him, told him the codicil would stand, and this had influenced him, making him knowingly or unknowingly more reluctant to disobey her wishes and marry Katie Sorel. "What of the other visits?"

"Not relevant, Chief Inspector. One was a matter of insurance. She hadn't read the small print in her policy and the company was refusing to pay the comparatively minor sum she was claiming for storm damage to her house. A letter from us and, without admitting liability, they paid for the sake of good relations."

"And the second?"

"Mrs Vail wanted to know how to get

rid of a sitting tenant in a house she owned — an old boy who's behind with the rent and trespasses on her land, but refuses to leave."

Tansey recognized the description as that of Bert Bilson and his cottage, or hovel as it had been called, but decided to let the Reverend Basil Moore deal with the problem of what was now to happen to Bert. He again thanked Waller-Clive for his cooperation, said goodbye and set off back to Kidlington.

The meeting with the solicitor had not been the waste of time he had expected. The lawyer, whom he had not at first meeting considered an impressive figure, had turned out to know what he was talking about and to be much more forthcoming than one of his older, more experienced partners might have been. And what he had had to say had not been useless.

Tansey was always interested to learn more about the victim of a crime, on the grounds that such knowledge often helped to point to the assailant. But on this occasion, he thought ruefully, he had merely strengthened the case against

Oliver Vail. He told himself that he must accept the evidence. He was becoming too personally involved, merely because of a small and beautiful autistic child who was no concern of his.

★ ★ ★

The press conference passed off reasonably well. In his opening statement Tansey stressed that it was little more than twenty-four hours since Mrs Vail's body had been found and the police were not magicians; some of the evidence was confusing. He gave them facts about the state of the sitting-room, the signs of struggle, the rifle, the estimated time of death, the missing jewellery, cash and possibly clothing, and the marks on a window sill which suggested that someone had climbed through. He concluded by saying that at the moment there was no definite suspect.

This was greeted by raucous laughter and a shout of "What about Oliver?" The questions had begun. Tansey admitted that Oliver Vail appeared to be missing and that the police would like to speak to him. He said that Mrs Vail's Jaguar was also missing — or stolen. Asked if he thought theft might be the motive for the whole crime, he agreed that it was a possibility. But the bulk of the questions centred on Oliver. Detective Chief Inspector Richard Tansey of the Thames Valley Police Serious Crime Squad might not know who had killed the Widow, but it was apparent to him that the media had made up its collective mind.

This view was strengthened when the press conference was brought to an end by the appearance of Sergeant Abbot with the spurious excuse that the Chief Inspector was wanted urgently on the telephone. Back in his office Tansey found on his desk a collection of cuttings from the day's press relating to Lydia Vail's death. Even before the press conference they all, without exception, while skirting the laws of libel, had fingered Oliver Vail. The *Colombury Courier* had a particularly damning article. A supposed but unidentified friend of Oliver's, apparently a colleague from the bank, had given the *Courier*'s reporter an interview in which he was alleged to have stated that Oliver was not like other men, that he was completely hag-ridden by his mother and if he had turned on her at last it was understandable.

Sighing, Tansey reached for his telephone. He spoke to Inspector Whitelaw, who was in the Incident Van at Little Chipping. Whitelaw had little to report. The milkman had wanted to deliver two pints of milk at eight o'clock that morning and had been turned away.

"He only delivers Mondays, Wednesdays and Fridays to the Vails," Whitelaw said. "That explains why Meg Denham never mentioned seeing bottles of milk left outside the back door, which would have alerted her that something might be wrong. There weren't any. If there had been she couldn't have failed to notice them and she'd probably have told you."

"One small mystery solved," said Tansey, who hadn't thought about milk deliveries, but saw no reason to admit it.

"Any other deliveries?"

"No post — like yesterday. The paper boy — actually a young man who drives a car — arrived at eight-forty, which he says is approximately his usual time. Yesterday he put the *Telegraph* through the letter-box — Mrs Vail didn't take the *Courier* — and went. He didn't see anyone."

"No. Meg Denham would have come, found the body, and fled, and the vicar and Corbet wouldn't have arrived yet. All very interesting, but really no damn use, is it?"

"Afraid not. But this might be useful. Vic Rowe, the gardener, turned up. He's a big, lumbering fellow, six foot and broad with it. He said he knew the Widow was dead, but that didn't mean the weeds would wait. I pointed out that there would be no one to pay him, but he said he was flush at the moment, and he'd trust Oliver to see him right when he got back."

"Nothing like having faith." Tansey was sarcastic. "Well, if that's all, Inspector — "

"No, sir." Whitelaw felt reproached. "Rowe was here on Wednesday afternoon.

That and Friday mornings are his regular times. He says he left at four-forty on Wednesday. He's positive it was four-forty, because he was meeting pals in Colombury later and had wanted to leave punctually to give himself time to clean up. However, he had arrived ten minutes late and — I quote — 'the old bitch' had made him make it up at the end of the afternoon before she would pay him. Incidentally he was paid in çash, so there was money in the house."

"That *is* interesting, if he's not telling lies. Of course, even if he left at four-forty he could have come back later, but that's not consistent with what we know of his character. He's the quick-tempered type, not the brooder. Get someone to check on him and the pals he was meeting."

"Will do. Any news of Oliver, sir?"

"Nothing useful, though every force in the country is looking for him and the Jaguar and his picture's in all the papers and will be on the television news at lunchtime. He's been sighted in various places, as always happens when someone's said to be missing, but there's no real lead."

"Still, he can't last long on two hundred pounds. He's used to his creature comforts. He wouldn't know how to rough it." Whitelaw was confident.

"If he sells the Jag he'll have a lot more than two hundred. He might not get a reasonable offer from a disreputable garage, but I suspect he wouldn't quibble. We ought to bear that in mind, though I don't want to start a wild goose chase over all the garages in the area. It would be different if we had some idea where he was heading."

"Yes, sir," said Whitelaw, thinking that Dick Tansey sounded depressed this morning. "Finding where he sold the car could certainly give us a trace on him."

"If we're lucky," Tansey said. He didn't feel lucky.

★ ★ ★

The Chief Inspector had lunch in the canteen. He was hungry, but the thought of the afternoon ahead of him watching Ghent cut up Lydia Vail's body ruined his appetite. Sergeant Abbot was waiting for him when he returned to his office.

"A fax from Forensic, sir," he said.

"Thanks."

Tansey took the fax and read it quickly. It was brief and to the point. There were several sets of fingerprints on the rifle with which Mrs Vail had been shot. They were too blurred for definite identification, except for those of the person who had last held the weapon and placed a finger on the trigger. These corresponded with Oliver Vail's; the others were probably Mrs Vail's, though, they repeated, they were too blurred to be definite. With regard to the blood types, they had been in touch with Dr Ghent.

"Well, that's pretty damning," Tansey said regretfully.

"Conclusive, sir?"

Tansey shrugged. "I would imagine so. But one thing's for sure: we've got to find this man, and fast."

"There's been another sighting, sir, and a more hopeful one. A woman telephoned to say she believes she travelled by train from Reading to Portsmouth yesterday afternoon with Oliver Vail. She was alone in a First Class carriage when this young man got in. He was wearing slacks and a jacket which didn't fit him very well, and he seemed nervous. She thought perhaps he didn't have a ticket, but when the inspector came around he produced one immediately, and it was First Class."

"Why didn't she phone yesterday?"

"She'd been on holiday and there was a lot to do when she got home, but when she saw a photograph of Oliver in her newspaper this morning she was convinced the young man on the train had been him, and felt she should do something about it. But why I said it was hopeful, sir, was because she saw him again on the boat, the Portsmouth to Ryde ferry — and he used to live on the Isle of Wight."

Tansey was surprised. "How did you know that, Abbot? I only learnt it myself from Mrs Vail's lawyer this morning."

"Katie Sorel told me when I drove her home yesterday. She said he had been brought up there. At the time I didn't think it important, but combined with this woman's recognition it might be, mightn't it?"

"Yes, indeed. Abbot, you get on the

blower to Inspector Whitelaw and tell him about this. We were just talking about Oliver selling the car. Now, if he left Reading by train he likely sold the Jaguar there, so we must concentrate on garages — we agreed on small and doubtful establishments — in that neighbourhood. Meanwhile, I'll prepare a fax for the Hampshire Force Headquarters and ask them about the Isle of Wight police. I think we can safely say now that Oliver Vail is wanted for questioning concerning the unlawful killing of his mother."

★ ★ ★

The post-mortem on Lydia Vail was less of an ordeal than Tansey had expected. Dr Ghent was his usual efficient self, but somewhat more subdued than usual. He made no attempt to give the Chief Inspector an anatomy lesson or to make semi-obscene jokes about the human body and its workings, but confined himself to a murmured dictation to his assistant — murmurs which Tansey found hard to hear or understand. He got through his business quickly, washed and offered Tansey coffee in his office.

"I assume you'd like a mini-report before the official one," he said.

"Please. Anything you can give me."

"Right. I can give you a fairly complete run-down, both on the body and the scene of crime, because I've been in touch with Forensic who have just finished dealing with the various blood and tissue samples."

"I know, they told me."

"Fine. Well, the body first. It was well-nourished and the lady took good care of herself. Her teeth were in excellent condition, or had been until the face was smashed. The nails were manicured. The hair was tinted. Age — in early sixties, which I think is confirmed by the birth certificate you found. She didn't spare money on herself or her clothes, which were all expensive."

None of this surprised Tansey. "Time and cause of death?" he prompted.

"Time, Wednesday, between five and eight in the evening. I can't be more accurate than that."

"Three hours," Tansey mused. "I

164

suppose you wouldn't be prepared to give an off the record guess at a closer time, would you?"

"No." Ghent was firm. "What's the point of asking for scientific investigation, if you're going to go ahead by guesswork anyway?"

"But you must have an opinion," Tansey persisted.

Ghent looked exasperated, but at last he said, "All right. For what it's worth, which is precious little, I think she was probably killed between six and seven, but I'm not swearing to that in any court."

"Thanks," Tansey said. "And cause?"

"She was battered to death with the rifle that was found beside her, and which is definitely the murder weapon. She was dead when she was shot by this same rifle. Forensic have already done the comparison tests, as you know, and both the bullets, including the one under the body, were fired from it."

"Yes," said Tansey.

"Now," Ghent went on, "there is another point. The rifle was fired from close enough to her head to get not only

165

her blood but particles of her tissue on it. What may be of more importance is that there's also foreign tissue on it."

"Foreign tissue? On the rifle?"

"Yes. Not Mrs Vail's. I would say it's safe to presume it comes from her assailant, and it should certainly help you to convict him once you catch him. So will the blood, though I must admit there's one anomaly. The samples from the carpets show that someone — presumably the murderer — went upstairs after she was dead and washed in the bathroom, but later came down and washed again in the cloakroom. At least there were a couple of particles of tissue — Mrs Vail's — on the side of the downstairs wash basin, but the spots of blood there and on the towel don't seem to equate with any other blood in the house. I can't explain this, except to suggest that someone — a visitor, servant, gardener — might have cut himself or herself earlier. But I doubt if the point is of importance. And that, Chief Inspector, is all I can tell you."

And, added to the rest of the

circumstantial evidence against him, it would be enough, Tansey thought as he drove back to Headquarters, to put Oliver Vail behind bars for a large number of years.

11

THE following day, Saturday, Detective Chief Inspector Tansey and Detective Sergeant Abbot returned to Little Chipping. Tansey had planned a series of interviews, hoping to coordinate some of the varied statements that had been made; but in order that the questions and answers should seem informal, he had given no warning of his intentions.

The detectives' first stop was at St Matthew's vicarage. "Saturday's a bad day for the vicar," Abbot had remarked. "He'll be writing his sermon for tomorrow."

"Probably cribs it straight from a book," Tansey said cynically. "Anyway, it's Janice Moore I want to talk to, though we'd better have an adult present too, and you must take notes for a statement for her to sign later, Abbot."

"Right, sir, though if you ask me that little madam's perfectly capable of

168

writing a statement for herself. However, here we are. At least I hope we are."

"I see why you think we may have come to the wrong place." Tansey laughed.

The reason for Abbot's doubt was a small van parked directly in front of the main door of the vicarage. It had clearly seen better days. The panelling was warped, there were strong signs of rust and a door was tied shut with string. But what had amused the two detectives was the psychedelic paintwork. The van had been sprayed with a variety of patterns and colours, and looked like a wall poster designed by an angry child or a graffito in a New York subway.

As Abbot parked behind it, Tansey said, "One wonders how such a vehicle ever managed to pass its MOT test." He got out of the car and walked around the van.

"What d'you think you're doing?"

Tansey jumped. A man had appeared behind him. The fact that he was carrying a hoe and was a big, shambling fellow, fitting the description that inspector Whitelaw had give of the gardener, assured Tansey that this was Vic Rowe.

"Ah, Mr Rowe," Tansey said. "I'm Chief Inspector Tansey and this is Sergeant Abbot."

"Police!" Rowe didn't actually spit, but he looked as if he were about to. "What do you want me for? I told that Inspector all I know."

"Actually, we've met you by chance, Mr Rowe. We came to see the vicar. We didn't expect you to be here."

"It's my morning for the vicarage. I'm always here of a Saturday."

"Well, we weren't aware of that. However, now we've met you, perhaps you'd confirm one or two facts for us. You say you left the Vails' house at four-forty on Wednesday evening."

"I did, and the old girl was in her usual nasty mean form, making me work my exact number of hours."

"Did you go into the downstairs cloakroom at any time that day?"

"Good Lord, no! I wasn't allowed in the house. There's an outside privy and that was good enough for the likes of me in her ladyship's eyes, though there was nowhere to wash."

"Then you went home and got ready

to meet your friends in Colombury. What time?"

"No particular time. It was Ken Coster's birthday, and a few of us agreed to meet at the Windrush and have a bite to eat, and then go on to a disco. Ken's a long-distance lorry driver, and he's not here that often."

"And when did *you* get to the pub?"

"About a quarter to seven. I was nearly the last of our lot to arrive."

"You mean it took you two hours to get ready for this party?"

"I found I'd got a slow puncture when I got back to my cottage, and the wheel wasn't easy to change. I had to take the van to Steve Overton's garage in the village. I'm dependent on the vehicle for my work. You can't cycle around carrying a lot of garden tools. Anyway, what's all these questions for?" Rowe glowered at Tansey. "If you think it was me who did in the Widow you'd better think again. Police!" And now he did spit, but wide of the Chief Inspector.

"Take it easy, Mr Rowe," Tansey said hurriedly before Abbot could intervene. "No one's accusing you of anything."

At this point, perhaps fortunately, Mrs Moore appeared at the front door and interrupted the conversation. She treated the three of them as friends. She welcomed Tansey and Abbot as if they had come to pay a social call or consult her husband on some knotty point of theology, and told 'Vic' that coffee was ready in the kitchen; Alan had just made it.

* * *

Following Grace Moore into a comfortable but surprisingly tidy living-room, Tansey thought that she was the ideal vicar's wife. He said, "Rowe was telling us he'd been to a party on Wednesday evening. I must say I find it difficult to imagine him at a disco."

"If you'd seen him all dressed up, you wouldn't be surprised," she said. "He's a good-looking man. A lot of the girls fancy him, but he still hankers after his lost love."

"His lost love?"

"Yes — Elaine from the Ploughman's. They even got as far as having the banns read. Then he gave her a black eye one night when he was drunk, and she called it off, though I think she's still fond of him." Grace Moore gave a wry smile. "But why am I rabbiting on like this? You're not interested in village gossip."

Tansey didn't contradict her. Gossip could be extremely useful, especially in confined districts like villages. He now knew why Elaine Pulman had denied that there was anyone in the area who had an erratically violent temper. She had at once thought of Vic Rowe, and for her sake the Corbets had remained silent too; this could possibly be important, though it was hard to see why.

"Mrs Moore, we've come here this morning to talk to Janice, if you'll allow us."

"Janice?"

Tansey explained. "Of course we'd like you to be present. These times when she saw Oliver Vail and heard shots could be absolutely vital, as I'm sure you appreciate."

Grace Moore nodded. "I'll fetch Jan." She hesitated. "Chief Inspector, you will remember she's only a child, won't you?"

Without waiting for a reply Mrs Moore left them, to return almost immediately with her daughter, who greeted Tansey warmly, and looked slightly suspiciously at Abbot who now had his notebook out in front of him. She made no comment, however.

"Hello, Inspector, Ma says you want to talk to me."

"Yes indeed, Miss Moore."

"You may call me Jan, Inspector."

"Detective Chief Inspector," Abbot corrected her as Tansey said, "Thank you."

"Detective Chief Inspector? Oh dear, that's an awful mouthful." Janice cocked her head on one side. "I suppose I couldn't call you Tansey, could I?"

While Sergeant Abbot made an incomprehensible sound at the back of his throat, Tansey laughed aloud. In his opinion Grace Moore's warning that her daughter was still only a child had been quite unnecessary. Nevertheless, that didn't mean that everything she said was always valid.

"OK," he said. "Call me what you like, Jan, but this is important. I want you to tell me once again, slowly and carefully, about Wednesday evening when you were in the woods behind the Vails' house. You saw Oliver?"

"Yes. I didn't see him come home, but I saw him leave, in what seemed to me a great hurry. He slammed the car door and took off."

"When was this?"

"Shortly after seven — before quarter past."

"Jan was home by seven twenty-five," her mother volunteered.

Tansey nodded his thanks to Mrs Moore for the confirmation and, to take Janice's mind off the time for the moment, asked, "What was he wearing?"

"His banking suit. Dark grey. He can't have changed since he came back from work."

"He could easily have had more than one dark suit," Mrs Moore pointed out.

Janice ignored the comment. "And I've been thinking, Tansey. You asked me before if he was carrying a bag and I said I didn't know, but when I remember him leaping into the car I'm almost positive he wasn't."

"That's interesting," Tansey said. "Now, Jan, other people? Forget Oliver for the moment."

"I only saw Miss Gore's lodger. He came running out of the woods, as I told you, a bit after six-thirty. He didn't go near the house. He was in casual clothes, slacks and a jacket." Janice grinned wickedly. "I wanted to see who would follow him, which is why I waited and saw Oliver. I thought he — the lodger, I mean — might have been with Elaine. Quick work, if so, I thought. And with his so-called wife just up the road."

"Janice!" her mother protested.

Janice ignored her. "Anyhow, I never saw her. I suppose she could have gone a different way down to the road. The woods are quite big."

"How long were you there that evening?" Tansey asked.

"In the woods? From about half past five till just after seven, as I said. But most of that time I wasn't near the Vails' house. I was seeing how many different kinds of wild flowers I could spot — for my nature notebook."

Janice Moore looked the Chief Inspector in the eye and smiled. He had no doubt that she remembered telling him that she had been spying on her brother Alan, whom she also suspected of meeting Elaine Pulman. She seemed to have some kind of fixation about the Ploughman's barmaid.

"You told me you heard shots," Tansey said, accepting the half-truth or whatever it was because of Grace Moore's presence. "What time would that have been?"

"I'm not sure." Janice shook her head.

"You get so used to hearing shots in the country," Grace Moore said, "rabbits or pigeons — or the odd fox. You don't really notice them, and on the whole it's better not to ask questions. They're not always legal, I'm afraid."

"Mrs Vail was shot, as well as being brutally assaulted," Tansey pointed out gently.

Grace Moore flushed. "I — I was trying to explain why — "

"Yes, I know."

"There was a shot not long before I set off for home," Janice said. "Half an hour perhaps. And I remember thinking it was

177

Bert Bilson, and I suppose it must have been because he brought Ma a rabbit next day. But there were some earlier — I think. Tansey, I'm sorry. I simply can't remember."

"That's all right, Jan. Much better to say you don't remember than produce a statement that could be misleading. As it is you've been a great help. Thank you both."

Tansey smiled from daughter to mother. He was pleased. The interview had been satisfactory. Jan hadn't contradicted anything she had said when he had first met her, and she had added more, possibly valuable, information.

★ ★ ★

"Where to now, sir?" Abbot asked his usual question as they left the vicarage.

"A brief visit to Miss Gore. Correct me if I'm wrong, Abbot, but didn't the pseudo Mrs Smith say that Miss Gore provided the evening meal at six-thirty. High tea, she called it scornfully."

"Yes, that's right, sir."

"Then we'll ask about the meal on

Wednesday evening. It'll be a check on one of Miss Moore's times. Incidentally, you were quite right about Jan. I shouldn't be surprised if she had her statement all neatly written out when we next see her."

Abbot snorted. "That child!" he said. "Wouldn't you know she'd be a parson's daughter?"

Tansey laughed. "She's a bright little girl. One could have a lot worse witness." Involuntarily he thought of Joy Sorel. Then, shaking his head, he said, "Do you remember which is Miss Gore's house, Abbot?"

"Yes, it's this one here."

Abbot drew up in front of a small square house. When they had been talking to the Smiths outside Miss Gores's gate on Thursday morning Tansey hadn't paid any attention to it. Now he regarded the neat strip of flowers bordering the path that led to the whitened step before the front door, the two patches of mown grass, the lace curtains, the gleaming brasswork of the knocker, letter-box and bellpush. From this and what he had been told about her, he drew a mental

179

picture of Miss Mary Gore, and she didn't disappoint him.

"Yes?" she asked bluntly, standing in her doorway.

Mary Gore was a tall, thin woman, with grey hair pulled back from a face that had once been pretty, but was now faded and sad and with a bitter mouth. Her expression was not welcoming, and didn't change when Tansey introduced himself and Abbot. She gave no indication that she was about to invite them into the house, and made it clear that whatever interview she was prepared to grant them would take place on the doorstep.

"Miss Gore, until last Thursday you had some lodgers who gave their names as Smith — "

"I don't take lodgers, Chief Inspector," she interrupted. "I take house guests in the summer, only two at a time and really as a favour. Inexpensive accommodation is difficult to find, and I like young people."

"I understand." The Chief Inspector, who hadn't in the least minded being called Tansey by Janice Moore, objected to being treated like a lowly police recruit by Mary Gore. "And presumably you have house rules, such as the hour they must be in at night and the need to be punctual for meals?" he said coldly.

"Naturally."

"What time do you serve the evening meal?"

Miss Gore's nostrils quivered at the word 'serve', which Tansey had used deliberately. "Six-thirty."

"Last Wednesday evening were Mr and Mrs Smith punctual for the meal? Please think carefully, Miss Gore."

Mary Gore hesitated. She disliked Tansey and she disliked his questions, which she considered impertinent, and she would gladly have lied, but Tansey's authoritative request to think carefully stopped her. It had sounded almost like a warning.

"Mrs Smith was punctual," she said. "Mr Smith was about fifteen minutes late. It was very annoying, but he apologized profusely. He explained that he had gone for a walk in the woods and had got lost. Now, if that's all, Chief Inspector, I — "

"Yes, that's all — for the moment, Miss

Gore. Thank you for your cooperation. Good morning."

Tansey turned away abruptly and, followed by Abbot who had muttered a good morning, made for the car. As he got in he saw that Miss Gore had already shut her front door. Damn the woman, he thought. Why couldn't she be civil? But he knew from past experience it was a mistake to let witnesses rile you, and a worse mistake to show it. It made them feel they had scored over you, with the consequence that a piece of evidence might be withheld out of mischief, or merely lost through ignorance of its potential importance.

"At least Miss Gore answered the major question, didn't she, sir?" said Abbot, replying to his unspoken thoughts. "She verified Janice Moore's evidence. Janice may be a precocious little brat, but she seems reliable."

"Yes, she does," Tansey agreed. "Let's go and see if Bert Bilson verifies it too."

★ ★ ★

They had trouble finding Bert Bilson's home because they didn't recognize it. Whoever had originally commissioned the Vails' house had had grandiose ideas, and had caused a small lodge to be built at the end of the drive. There were no gates to be opened and shut, and no sign that there had ever been any, so it was possible that the lodge had been meant for show, and had never been intended for human habitation. Indeed, since it had been allowed to fall into disrepair, it was even more difficult to believe that anyone was living there now.

When they had stopped and asked a small boy where Mr Bilson lived Abbot thought the child was pulling his leg, but Steve Overton, the local garage owner, had confirmed it. Since his wife had died fifteen years ago Bert Bilson had lived alone in the lodge, but it was only after Mrs Vail had settled into the house that he had been forced to pay any rent.

"It's a dreadful place," Overton said. "My wife went inside once when Bert was ill, and she said it wasn't fit for a beast. The Widow's done nothing to improve it, and yet she had the nerve to charge him for it. The joke is that when she really got stroppy with Bert, Oliver used to pay the rent for him without telling her."

Tansey shook his head when Abbot recounted this story. "If Oliver Vail comes to trial for his mother's murder there had better not be too many good men — or women — and true from Little Chipping and the district on the jury, or he'll be acquitted before they start the proceedings."

Abbot laughed. "One thing's for sure. He won't be wanting for character witnesses. Not that they'll do him much good," he added soberly.

"Not with the way the evidence is shaping up," Tansey agreed, "but they might help. He could plead diminished responsibility due to a brainstorm or something, and, given a good barrister and an understanding judge, he could be put away for as little as ten — even five — years. On the other hand he could get a life sentence; after all, it was a brutal killing."

Such was British justice, Tansey thought, no worse than in many countries and better than in most. And here was another example — this so-called lodge, this place 'not fit for a beast' that Mrs Vail had described to her solicitor, Waller-Clive, as a 'house'. Watching Abbot banging on the paint-stripped front door, Chief Inspector Dick Tansey was thankful that the disposition of justice was not his direct affair.

"No answer, sir," said Abbot, returning to the car.

"Right. Then we'll go to the Ploughman's and have a drink. It's past opening time."

★ ★ ★

The first person they saw on entering the pub was the bandy-legged little man whom Tansey recognized, from the time he had seen him at the vicarage, as Bert Bilson. Bert was staring sadly into the last inch of beer in his glass, but cheered up at once when Tansey offered him another.

"Would that be a pint or a half, Chief Inspector?" asked Sidney Corbet, grinning broadly from behind the bar,

185

and winking. "It were a half before."

"A pint," Bilson said, forestalling Tansey. "It's not often as the police buy me a beer. They must be wanting something."

"A few questions," Tansey said.

Bilson groaned, but he willingly followed Tansey to a corner table where they could talk without interruption. Elaine brought them their drinks — halves for Tansey and Abbot and a pint for Bert Bilson — and when Abbot told her she was looking very smart she nodded towards two men seated at the far end of the bar.

"Press!" she murmured. "There were a lot more yesterday, asking questions about Oliver and the Widow, and taking photographs. I'm expecting my picture to appear in one of the Sundays." She beamed with pleasure.

"Before you go, Miss Pulman," Tansey said, "can you recall any jewellery that Mrs Vail used to wear?"

"Jewellery? No. But I scarcely knew her. She never came in here."

"Fair enough. Would you ask Mrs Corbet if she remembers any?"

"Sure."

Surprisingly, as Elaine departed, Bert Bilson said, "I can tell you. The Widow had a whole set of jewellery made of shiny black stuff — jet, it's called. Mostly she wore that, but she had a couple of gold chains and a lovely diamond brooch and some pearls."

"You seem to have known her pretty well, Mr Bilson." Tansey was amused.

"Too darned well. She was always on at me about one thing or another. Her latest was to try to get rid of me altogether, to drive me out of a place that's been my home for years." He shook his head in disgust and took a long swallow of his beer. "But it weren't me that put the dead cat on her doorstep, if that's what you were going to ask me. I reckon it was one of the kids from the village."

"Actually I wasn't going to ask you anything about the cat, Mr Bilson, but about Wednesday evening, when I believe you were shooting rabbits in the woods."

"No, I weren't. All day Wednesday I was up at Farmer Price's t'other side of Colombury, helping with his fencing.

You can ask him. It was around eight when his son brought me back. Delivered me to m'door, he did, after Mrs Price had given me supper. Kind people, the Prices. Not like some."

Tansey looked inquiringly at Abbot, who nodded. "Yes. I know Bill Price," he said. "Good chap, sir. Perhaps he gave Mr Bilson a couple of rabbits and Mr Bilson sold one of them to Mrs Moore the next day."

"No, he didn't. I went rabbiting early Thursday morning. That's the best time to catch the little beggars unawares."

Bert Bilson drained his glass and looked meaningfully at Tansey, who gestured to Corbet that Bert would like a refill, and Elaine came over with a fresh pint.

"Rose can't remember anything about Mrs Vail's jewellery," she said. "Is it important?"

"Not really," Tansey said. "I think we have enough information already."

"I could ask Katie." Elaine was eager to help. "I'll be seeing her this afternoon. She's making me a new dress for the big end of month disco."

There was a burst of laughter from

three young men who had come to occupy the next table and had heard the last part of the conversation. "And who's taking you to the dance, sweetie — Vic Rowe?" one of them inquired.

Elaine glared at them, and then deliberately turned her back.

"Men! Those are just yokels," she said in disgust. But she evidently didn't include Tansey in that kind of category for she leant towards him and added, "Would you believe it? Tom Sorel wants Katie to take him back! Keeps on pestering her, he does. And after all she's been through, with his womanizing and his failure to give her any money, in spite of what the divorce court said, and his threats if she married Oliver. He's always been madly jealous of her, but it didn't matter what he did himself. He even tried it on with me once. The Smasher!" She made a sound of obvious disgust.

"All men aren't like that," Abbot protested.

"Maybe not, but it's best to keep one's independence."

Sidney Corbet was calling to Elaine

that he needed her help. The bar was filling up Tansey thanked Bilson for answering his questions so frankly, and waved goodbye to Corbet. Abbot was hopefully eyeing the plates of sandwiches that Rose had just brought in, and Tansey hesitated.

Then he made up his mind and went to the door, showing signs of impatience. "I'm sorry," Tansey said as they reached their car. "But now for Price's farm. I'm pretty sure Bilson was telling the truth but we'd better check on him, and a farmer's likely to be back from the fields and having his midday meal now. Our own lunch can wait till we get back to HQ, Abbot."

"Yes, sir," said Abbot, thinking regretfully that the Windrush Arms would have done splendidly in place of sandwiches from the Ploughman's Arms, and have been much better than the police canteen.

12

THEORETICALLY the Chief Inspector had a rest day due to him. This didn't mean that on the Sunday he was not on call should Inspector Whitelaw, who was the senior officer in charge of the Vail case in Tansey's absence, consider it necessary to summon him. For anyone as conscientious as Dick Tansey it was not exactly a relaxing arrangement.

However, he did his best to play the part of loving husband and father. He brought Hilary breakfast in bed, he entertained his young son, he mowed the lawn, he did one or two odd jobs about the house — jobs about which Hilary had been nagging him for weeks. But all this occupied only three-quarters of his mind; the other quarter was busy wondering about Oliver Vail — where he might be, what he might be doing, how he might be feeling, whether he was thinking of giving himself up, or even taking his own life.

Tansey knew that if Oliver had in fact been found, or if there had been any important breakthrough in the case, Whitelaw would have been on the phone at once. He was therefore waiting for it to trill, and when it did — first, his father asking if there was any hope of a visit; then Hilary's sister just wanting to chat — he had to restrain himself, both from dashing to answer it and from intervening to cut the conversation short. Though he wouldn't have admitted it, he was thankful when the so-called rest day was over.

On Monday, which luckily was not to be without incident, he arrived at his Kidlington office early, shuffled through his in-tray, and waited impatiently for Inspector Whitelaw, whom he had arranged to meet at a specific time, to appear. Whitelaw was late. He apologized.

"I'm sorry, sir, but I've not been idle. Yesterday was uneventful. Still no news of Oliver Vail or the Jaguar, though the country's forces are doing their best."

"It doesn't seem to be a very good best; certainly it's not yielding much in the way of results," said Tansey sourly.

"Unfortunately not, sir. It's the same everywhere — a question of shortage of men, sir. It takes a lot of manpower to make these time-consuming inquiries. The only thing is to get lucky — and we haven't been lucky yet. And, let's face it, we can't expect the Northumberland Force or the Scots, say, to be as interested in the case as we are."

"I know." Tansey sighed. He hadn't meant to be critical, but he was worried that Oliver, who had never been on the run in his life before, had managed to elude the authorities for so long; the car was less important — if more easily identifiable — merely a means to the end of locating Oliver. "I suppose all we can do is hope today will be more fruitful."

"There's a good chance it already has, which is why I'm late. A Mr Paul Dale, who's been staying with his mother outside Colombury, took his dog for a walk before breakfast this morning. The dog incidentally is a dachshund — you know, a badger hound, used to holes. According to its owner it was normally obedient, but today it ran off and didn't come back when he called. He found it trying to pull something out of a rabbit hole — a shirt and a pair of jeans, both apparently stiff with blood."

Even the prosaic Maurice Whitelaw couldn't resist the temptation of pausing for effect before he continued. "Mr Dale is a London lawyer and a bright young man. He knew about Lydia Vail's murder and he knew that no one pushes bloody clothes down a rabbit hole without a reason. He said they weren't old and looked as if they hadn't been there long. So they're on their way to Forensic, sir."

"That's splendid. Of course, there could be an element of coincidence." Tansey paused and frowned. "I find it hard to imagine Oliver coming home in his dark banking suit, changing into casuals, killing his mother, and then calmly putting on another suit, don't you?"

"There were clothes strewn all over his room, sir, as you've seen from the reports," Whitelaw reminded the Chief Inspector, "and he had a whole row of suits. If he was in a hurry, as presumably he was, he might have seized on any one of them. He was used to wearing suits, after all."

Tansey grunted. "Sure. Then he drives off until he finds a convenient field and stuffs the blood-stained clothes down a hole? Ah well, murderers do strange things in the heat of the moment and its aftermath. Anyway, once Forensic get to work we'll soon know whether these clothes are Oliver's or not — or at least we'll know the identity of the blood on them, which I'd assume is Mrs Vail's. You've got the lawyer's name and address, of course?"

"Yes, sir, and I'm having a statement typed for him right now. He's promised to look in on his way back to London to sign it."

"Good!"

"Donaldson has cordoned off the area of the rabbit hole, and I've sent a couple of men out there to see if they can find tyre marks or anything interesting, but I've not much hope of that. It's rough ground and much used."

"Nevertheless." Tansey nodded his approval of Whitelaw's efficiency — not surprising the Inspector had been late reporting at HQ — Tansey had a passing thought that he must take a proper holiday; he knew he was becoming hypercritical and short-tempered and this was clouding his judgement. "Who knows? We may well have reason to be grateful to Mr Paul Dale, Inspector."

"Yes — and to his dog, sir," said Whitelaw with an unexpected flash of humour.

★ ★ ★

Later in the morning a Mr Thane telephoned Headquarters and asked to speak to Detective Chief Inspector Tansey. He said it was in connection with the murder of Mrs Vail, who was a customer of his, and he believed he had some valuable information to offer.

"Who's Mr Thane?" asked Tansey of the police officer who had asked if he would take the call.

"Thane and Sons, fishmongers and poulterers in the Oxford market, sir. I'd say it's a pretty thriving business."

"And Mrs Vail was a customer? OK.

Have him put through to me right away."

To judge from his voice on the phone Mr Thane was a purposeful character. "You are Detective Chief Inspector Tansey?" he demanded at once. "You're the senior officer in charge of this case?" And when Tansey admitted that this was so, he said, "Good. I always believe in going to the top."

Tansey smiled to himself as he thought of the hierarchy above him, but said, "You have some information for me, I gather, Mr Thane," hoping that the fishmonger and poulterer wasn't wasting everybody's time.

"Yes. I'm sorry not to have contacted you before, but my wife's mother died and we've been away for several days and had other problems on our minds. However, this is the point. I called on Mrs Vail on Wednesday evening. I'm not in the habit of delivering produce myself but — it was like this — "

According to Thane, Mrs Vail had come into the shop on Wednesday morning. She wanted to buy a duck, but he was not expecting any ducks to be delivered until the afternoon.

She had said he could send one over when they arrived; she needed it early the next day. Thane's did have a van which made deliveries to Colombury and various Cotswold villages twice a week, but Wednesday was not one of those days. With many apologies he had explained that unfortunately this would be impossible, and Mrs Vail had become indignant. She had said that either Mr Thane delivered a duck before six-thirty that evening, or in future she would take her custom elsewhere.

"Then she stalked out of the market," Thane said with a great sigh. "Of course I could have done nothing about it. I admit I was sorely tempted, but Mrs Vail was an excellent customer and no one can afford to throw away business these days. So I swallowed my pride, Chief Inspector. When the ducks came in I put a beauty aside and decided to take it around myself."

"What time did you get there, Mr Thane?"

"Six-twenty. I was held up by one of those damned farm machines and I was afraid I wouldn't make it before Mrs

Vail's deadline, but I did — just."

"And?" Tansey inquired.

"I rang the back doorbell. It spluttered but didn't seem to work very well which irritated me, and I kept my thumb on it. Then I heard a lot of water coming through the pipes into the drain and I thought Mrs Vail might have been having a bath. I was in a quandary. Having made the effort to deliver the wretched bird I wasn't going to take it away again, but I couldn't just leave it on the doorstep. It was a warm evening, and there was a chance cats might get at it. I waited. Still no one answered the doorbell — I doubt if she could hear it. I tried the back door, not expecting it to be unlocked, but it was, so I went into the kitchen and put the duck into the refrigerator. I was only in the house for a couple of minutes. But I suppose that what I'm telling you, Chief Inspector, is that Mrs Vail was alive at six-twenty or twenty-five."

"Mr Thane, you don't know that it was Mrs Vail you heard. You didn't see her, did you?"

"No. I didn't see anyone, but — "

"It could have been Mr Oliver Vail."

Thane was quick on the uptake. "But — but — you mean, he might have just murdered her and was washing off the blood? Oh my God, I never thought of that!"

Tansey didn't answer the question. He allowed Thane a moment to get over the shock of possibly having been so near to the murderer, the murderer whom he had naturally assumed, from what he had learnt through the media, to be Oliver Vail. Then Tansey said, "Did you see a car, any kind of vehicle near the house?"

"No. I didn't pass anything on the drive, and there was nothing parked outside."

"I suppose you didn't look in the garage?"

"No. Why should I? Even if it had been open I couldn't have left the duck there. She might not have found it."

"Quite." Tansey didn't explain why the question was less stupid than it had appeared to Thane.

"But I'll tell you what I did find, which was odd. There was a man's tie lying on the ground not far from the back door. Not silk, but a good quality tie, dark blue with red spots. I've one rather like it myself. I thought it could have been Oliver's but I couldn't be bothered with it. However, it was still there when I came out of the house — as one might have expected — and being a tidy individual I picked it up and carefully hung it over a rhododendron bush where anyone could see it."

"Yes, that is odd," Tansey agreed, thinking that the real oddity was that no one who had been at the Vails' early on Thursday morning had mentioned a tie hanging on a bush.

He dismissed the thought; there were always oddities in any case. He thanked Thane for his information, warned him that they would probably need an official statement from him, and said goodbye. Then he sat at his desk, staring straight ahead of him.

Thane's evidence had to be accepted; no one would doubt it. Therefore at about six-thirty on Wednesday evening either Lydia Vail was still alive or her murderer was in the house. However, there had been no car outside, and therefore Oliver had not yet arrived. Why not? He had left Field's garage by six o'clock.

Tansey again reached for the phone. He had suddenly remembered that he hadn't asked Jan Moore about the car. She had said she hadn't seen Oliver arrive, and carelessly he had taken it for granted that Oliver was already at home when she saw Paul Smith, Miss Gore's lodger, come running out of the woods shortly after six-thirty.

"Jan, more questions, I regret to say," he said when she had been brought to the telephone in the vicarage.

"That's OK, Tansey. I hope I can answer them."

"You told me you saw Paul Smith, Miss Gore's lodger, hurrying from the woods? Did you notice if the Vails' Jaguar was there then?"

"I'm sure it wasn't, or I'd have seen it."

"So Oliver arrived after Smith had gone." Tansey was thinking aloud. "About six forty-five."

"Yes, he must have done," Jan said.

She sounded doubtful, and Tansey pounced on her doubt. "But you said earlier that after you'd seen Smith go you watched for Elaine. How could you have missed Oliver's arrival?"

There was silence at the other end of the line. Then in a small voice Jan said, "I had to go and pee. I'd wanted to before I saw Smith, and I couldn't wait any longer. I nipped into a — a secluded place I know. I was only there a minute or two, but when I got back the car was there, so Oliver must have arrived. I should have told you all this before."

"Why should you?" Tansey said consolingly. "The point didn't occur to me to ask you until a few minutes ago, Jan. But it's brought up another thing. You said you heard a shot not long before you set off home. You put it at about an hour before. But would it have been before or after you saw Smith?"

"After, but not long after."

"That's fine. That's what I wanted to know. Many thanks, Jan."

★ ★ ★

When Inspector Whitelaw came into Chief Inspector Tansey's office in the mid-afternoon, he found Tansey standing in front of his wall blackboard, which was covered with figures and letters.

"What on earth — sir?" he said, hiding his amusement.

"You're just the man I want," said Tansey. "Here's a scenario for you." He pointed to the blackboard. "You pick holes in it."

"If I understand it — "

Tansey laughed. "It's not difficult, though it's taken me a fair while to work it out. The figures are times, the letters are people's initials. I'll explain."

"Oliver left Katie at 5.50 and went to Field's garage. He left there at six. He drove around, upset because Katie had given him an ultimatum; he had to choose between her and his mother. He arrived home at 6.40 — see. Jan Moore is the witness to this time. By then Thane, the poulterer, had come and gone, having heard water running at 6.25, so presumably Mrs Vail was

204

alive then. Oliver and his mother quarrel. He kills her, washes off the blood — I wish we knew his blood group — puts on a different suit, seizes what cash and jewellery he can and drives off at 7.10. Time thanks to Jan again." Tansey looked inquiringly at Whitelaw. "What do you think?"

"If I were the defence counsel," Whitelaw said slowly, "I'd have to accept that Oliver had motive, means and opportunity, and it looks bad that he bolted. However, I would defy anyone to believe that he could have accomplished all you've suggested in half an hour. It isn't practical, sir, not even if he went straight into the house, collected the rifle and started in on her right away. You've got to give them time for some argument — longer if the argument grows this heated. Of course, if I were prosecuting I'd do my damned best to shake those times."

Tansey nodded. "They're not foolproof, but I'd trust them within five minutes either way. Nevertheless, I take your point. They'll have to be checked and rechecked. What worries me is how he managed to cleanse himself of all the blood so quickly."

"Yes, indeed, sir — and I have news. The Jaguar has been traced to a garage outside Reading. It's been impounded and is on its way to Forensic, but in the meantime there are said to be no obvious signs of blood in it, and the garage owner — who bought it last Thursday — though admittedly not a very reputable character, swears it hasn't been near a car wash."

"Well, that certainly is news at last. Why didn't you tell me before?"

"I — I didn't have much chance, sir."

Tansey grinned. "Nor you did," he agreed and thought that there was one possibility that hadn't occurred to the Inspector; assuming the times were as accurate as he believed, Oliver Vail might have found his mother dead, panicked and fled. But then, who *had* killed her?

13

"I'M sorry we weren't quicker locating that Jaguar for you, Chief Inspector," Inspector Hamilton of the Reading Division of the Thames Valley Police Force apologized. "But you know as well as I do how it is — the increase in crime, shortage of staff, inexperienced men on the beat. All the usual excuses." Mocking himself, Hamilton grinned at Tansey, whom he had known for a number of years and both liked and respected.

"I do indeed," said Tansey, who in his turn appreciated Hamilton's discerning mind.

The two men seated in Hamilton's office, drinking tea and discussing the Vail case. They were alone, as Tansey had driven himself to Reading.

"Tell me about the garage proprietor," he said. "Is he an honest man?"

Hamilton grimaced. "He's never been in any trouble with the police, but anyone who buys and sells used cars leads a life of temptation, even if it's only in a small way. Personally I wouldn't go bail for Ted Shoeman, but I must emphasize that we've got nothing against him."

"How did he react to having the Jag removed?"

"As you'd expect, sir. With indignation. He's bought the car in good faith. He had studied Vail's credentials and the car's papers with great care to make sure the vehicle wasn't stolen. What more could he have done? He couldn't know it was involved in a murder case. And now who was to recompense him for the money he's paid for it?"

"I can imagine the scene," Tansey said. "Well, I better go and talk to him. That's why I'm here."

★ ★ ★

There was no problem in finding Shoeman's garage, because Hamilton had arranged for one of his uniformed officers to act as Tansey's driver in a marked police car. This was fortunate, for otherwise Tansey would have had difficulty in finding the place. It was on the outskirts of Reading and in a side road. It did have a couple of petrol pumps, but seemed to consist mainly of a large car lot. Mr Field of the Windrush Garage would have spurned it, but Tansey could see why Oliver Vail, cruising around trying to find somewhere to sell the Jag, had been thankful to happen upon it.

Ted Shoeman came out to greet them as they drove up, already eyeing the police insignia with interest. He was a short, square man with a wide smile that didn't hide some anxiety, and which disappeared completely when Tansey produced his warrant card and introduced himself.

"I've told the police all I know," Shoeman said sulkily.

"Mr Shoeman, I'm not interested in your business affairs. This is not a question of a stolen car; it's a case involving the particularly brutal murder of an elderly lady. In the circumstances the police have every right to ask for your full cooperation — and I mean full. So will you please take me to an office — somewhere we can talk."

It was an order, not a request, and Shoeman didn't quibble further. He led the way to a small, shabby room, furnished with a desk, a couple of chairs and a filing cabinet. Tansey pulled up a chair and sat down.

"Now, Mr Shoeman, we know that last week you bought a nearly-new Jaguar — so new that it was still under warranty. You say you've told other officers about it, but I want the story first hand. When did you buy it? Which day?"

"Thursday. He was waiting when I arrived at the lot about nine o'clock. He was in a dark suit, shirt and tie. He looked as if he was on his way to an office. A lawyer perhaps, or an accountant. I was surprised when he said he wanted to sell the Jag. By his appearance I wouldn't have thought he needed the money."

"Didn't that make you suspicious?"

"Sort of. But he gave me his name — Oliver Vail — and he had his driving licence, registration papers and all the other papers to show that the car belonged to him. He even had an account from a Colombury garage saying some minor work had been done on it the day before."

"But the car did *not* belong to him."

"So you say, but how was I to know? Everything was in order. As far as I could see, the car was the property of L. O. Vail and Oliver Vail was Lionel Oliver Vail. Was I expected to ask what his mother's initials were?"

Tansey ignored the question, and said, "Let's make sure of the identification." He produced half a dozen photographs from his pocket and spread them out before Shoeman. "Can you see him among this lot? Was he one of these?"

"That's the man," Shoeman said at once, pointing to Oliver Vail's picture.

"I see," replied Tansey. "Good. Now, did you ask him why he was selling the car?"

"Yes, and he told me to mind my own business. It did occur to me that perhaps he'd been involved in a hit-and-run accident, and because of that I examined the car carefully, but there was no sign of any trouble, no blood inside or out, nothing suspicious, and I decided to buy."

"How much did you give him?"

"Fifteen thousand. That's not a bad price. A Jag, like any other vehicle, loses a third of its original value almost as soon as it leaves the showroom. Ask any dealer."

"I believe you," said Tansey. "You gave him fifteen thousand pounds for the car. How? A cheque? You don't keep that kind of money in this place, do you?"

"I wish it had been by cheque. Then I could have stopped it. As it is I'm fifteen grand out of pocket. But he insisted on cash. Either cash, or the deal was off, he said. He drove me round to my bank. I got the money. Practically cleaned out my account, it did. We settled the transaction in the car, when I got him to sign the DVLC papers and so on. He got out and I drove back here in what I believed was my Jaguar — or would be as soon as the paperwork had been dealt with. Now all I'm left with is a chitty from the police saying they've taken it."

"Did Oliver Vail give you any idea where he might be heading?"

"None. We didn't have a social conversation."

"You bought the Jaguar on Thursday morning. Right?"

"Yes. I told you — and the other cops when they came."

"Why didn't you contact the police immediately when you learnt they were looking for a Jaguar that answered the description of the one you'd bought, *and* that they wanted to speak to a Mr Oliver Vail?"

"Because I didn't have time!"

"Mr Shoeman! You bought the Jaguar on Thursday morning and — "

"I know, I know, but it was like this, see."

Shoeman's story was that he had considered keeping the Jaguar for himself, as he didn't have a personal car at the moment. Of course, it would depend on whether he got a good offer, but meanwhile — Because of this possibility he had put the Jaguar, which was in perfect condition and immaculately clean, in a lock-up garage he owned. He had not been feeling too well. By the evening he was down with the summer flu that was going around. His partner was visiting her parents so he was alone, and had to look after himself. Anyhow, it wasn't until he listened to the news on Sunday, when he was beginning to improve, that he realized he had been duped. He had intended to call the police then, but when he came into the garage this morning the fuzz was all over the place already.

Tansey would have bet that the story was a mixture of lies and half-truths, but he didn't care. Here was the first genuine trace of Oliver Vail, and the Jaguar, however immaculate it had looked to a non-professional eye, should yield more information to Forensic. This was all to the good. The bad news was that Oliver now had a large sum of money in cash at his disposal, and had shown himself to be quick and resourceful. Nevertheless, the money wouldn't last for ever, and then his luck would run out. But they needed to catch him before that, Tansey thought — before he did something desperate.

★ ★ ★

When he saw the Chief Inspector leave the garage's office the young police constable got out of the car and opened

214

the door for him. "Inspector Hamilton has been on the blower with a message, sir," he said, indicating the radiophone.

"A message for me?"

"Yes, sir. A pawnbroker's on Castle Street has phoned in. He believes he may have bought some stolen jewellery, including a brooch which seems to fit the description of the one that belonged to Mrs Vail, by mistake."

"By mistake?" Tansey laughed.

"Well, as you know, we do issue regular and quite detailed lists of missing property, believed stolen. He says he only checked the latest list, which was issued two days after the murder, this morning, and realized he'd bought this brooch last week. It's fairly distinctive, I gather."

"Yes, I believe so. Inspector Hamilton gave you the name and address?"

"Yes, sir. He suggested we might go straight there, that is if you'd like to. It's more or less on the way back to the station."

"That's an excellent suggestion. Let's go."

★ ★ ★

The pawnbroker was a man in his early forties with a thin intelligent face and an efficient manner. He summoned a younger pale-faced woman, whom Tansey took to be his wife, to keep shop, and led the Chief Inspector into a back room.

"I didn't expect someone of your rank, Chief Inspector," he said easily. "I haven't got one of the Crown Jewels, have I?"

"Not quite, Mr Grove," Tansey said, "but you might have something of more immediate value. If the brooch was the property of Mrs Lydia Vail it might help to convict her killer. You've heard about the Vail case?"

"Yes, I have. There are a great many murders these days, and I usually avoid reading about them, but I was interested because my brother runs an antique shop in Colombury, close to Little Chipping, and I'm familiar with that part of the Cotswolds. And you really think this brooch — Dear God! I've never met a murderer before, at least as far as I know. I should say I don't normally buy many goods; I'm primarily a pawnbroker and I accept property as pledges against loans, but like most other pawnbrokers we do buy and sell occasionally, and in this case the chap was insistent I should buy the brooch and the rest of the stuff."

"You may not have met a murderer yet, Mr Grove," remarked Tansey.

He took out his little pile of photographs again and spread them out in front of the pawnbroker. Grove studied them in silence, then shook his head.

"No, my customer wasn't any of these."

"You're sure?"

"Quite sure."

Tansey was intrigued, but didn't show it. He reverted to Grove's earlier comment. "The rest of the stuff? There was more — apart from the brooch?"

"Yes. He said it all belonged to his mother, but he had no use for it as he didn't have a wife and he'd rather have the money. Wait a minute, Chief Inspector."

Grove went to a desk in a corner of the room and took out a manila envelope. Then he put a piece of velvet on the table beside Tansey and laid various pieces of jewellery on it. There were not more than half a dozen pieces.

"That Victorian brooch seems to fit the description we have," Tansey said, pointing. "Those two intertwined diamond hearts are distinctive, but for the rest I wouldn't know. We have no inventory of Mrs Vail's jewellery. Her son would recognize them, I suppose, but unluckily at the moment he's not available."

"Would it help if I described what I did *not* buy from this man?"

"It might." Tansey was cautious.

"Several gold chains. We've so many in the shop we don't want any more; the same applies to cultured pearl necklaces. He also offered me some jet pieces. The jet tempted me, I must admit, but it's not fashionable at present and, trade being what it is, I can't afford to put too much money into stock."

"Mr Grove, that's great, really helpful!" Tansey was pleased. "Everyone's spoken of Mrs Vail's predilection for jet and gold chains, and a pearl necklace has been mentioned too. I think it's safe to assume this is her missing jewellery."

Grove nodded. "I was afraid of that. Your good luck, Chief Inspector. My bad luck."

"Perhaps not. You may be compensated. In the meantime I'll have to take it all. Would you make out a receipt for me to sign?"

"Yes, of course. This is my own fault," Grove admitted as he itemized the jewellery on the receipt. "I should have read, learnt and inwardly digested your missing property list as soon as it came in. Then I'd have recognized the jewellery when this chap produced it. Mind you, I would have had no reason to connect it with the Vail killing, which could have been a piece of luck. He might have done for me too."

"Would you describe this character — and indeed the whole transaction?"

"It was eleven o'clock, Friday morning. I don't need to look it up. I remember because I'd opened the shop late and he was my first customer."

"Friday?"

Tansey was not surprised, since it was clearly not Oliver who had sold the jewellery to the pawnbroker. Oliver had been in Reading the day after his mother had been killed because he had sold the Jaguar on the Thursday morning. That was the last positive identification, but the lady who had travelled from Reading to Portsmouth with someone whom she thought might have been Oliver that afternoon, and had subsequently seen him on the ferry to the Isle of Wight, had unhesitatingly picked him out from a selection of photographs. However, Oliver could easily have sold the jewellery to someone he had met casually in some pub before he went to the Isle of Wight.

"He was a tall, confident, good-looking man," Grove said, "around thirty, with a rather ungainly walk."

"What sort of colouring?"

"Darkish brown hair. Blue-grey eyes. I'm sorry, Chief Inspector, I wasn't paying as much attention as I should have been. I'm not usually vague, but I'd just taken my wife to hospital for some tests. She's not at all well and I was worrying about her. For that matter I still am. However, my personal problems don't concern you, and I don't want to make them an excuse for not knowing what was on your damned list."

Tansey nodded his sympathy. "You'd know him if you saw him again?"

"Yes, I believe I would, unless he'd changed his appearance — dyed his hair or lost weight. He had a rather fat face."

"What about his voice? Any accent?"

"Quite well spoken. What I would call lower middle class." Grove stopped. "He spoke with a sort of burr, not very noticeable, but it was there. I've a good ear and at the time he reminded me of someone, and now I know. It wasn't anyone in particular. It was that Oxfordshire burr you hear in the Cotswolds."

Tansey stared at him. "Are you sure of that, Mr Grove? It could be vital."

"Well, I wouldn't bet my life on it. As I said before I wasn't at my best on Friday morning, but I'm pretty certain. I suppose I must have absorbed the fact subconsciously."

"Can you remember anything else about his appearance. Again, it could be terribly important. Please try."

"Let me think." Grove put a hand over his eyes and concentrated. "He was wearing grey slacks, a white T-shirt, a checked jacket, smart but not fancy — the sort of casual clothes I might easily buy for myself. He had a bit of sticking plaster on his forehead, said he'd got a bad scratch from a climbing rose. Honestly, that's all I can remember."

"What about his hands? His nails?"

Grove grinned and shook his head. "I'm sorry, Chief Inspector. You expect too much of me."

"You haven't done badly, Mr Grove. And I'm afraid you'll have to go through it again when you make your formal statement. We'll be in touch."

★ ★ ★

In fact, the pawnbroker had done wonderfully well, Tansey thought when, having expressed his thanks and said goodbye to Inspector Hamilton, he had collected his own car and was driving back to Oxford. For Grove had run out of his shop and banged on the window of the police car as the uniformed officer was about to pull away from the kerb.

"I've just this second remembered, Chief Inspector," he said excitedly. "As this chap was pointing to one of the pieces his sleeve rode up, and I saw he had a tattoo on his lower arm. I couldn't describe it. He pulled his sleeve down at once, but I'd swear it was a tattoo."

The suspicion crossed Tansey's mind that Grove had stressed his vagueness on Friday morning and his worry about his wife in order to excuse his carelessness in buying stolen goods. Surely a man in his line needed to be constantly observant and on guard against doubtful customers. But Grove's cooperation, and this added fact suggested that the suspicions were pointless. What was important was the evidence the pawnbroker had provided.

He had identified the seller of Lydia Vail's jewellery as a tall, good-looking man of about thirty with brown hair and blue-grey eyes and an ungainly walk. This description could have fitted innumerable men, but the Oxfordshire burr narrowed the field. Then the fact that he had blamed a climbing rose for the damage to his forehead was perhaps indicative of a gardener. Chief Inspector Tansey thought that if Vic Rowe had a tattoo on his right lower arm, he might have a lot of explaining to do.

14

THE telephone rang while the Tanseys were at breakfast. Hilary answered it. She returned, making a face.

"I don't need to tell you. It was the duty officer at Kidlington."

"I was afraid of that." Tansey hurriedly buttered a piece of toast and spread marmalade on it. "What did he want?"

"You, of course. Apparently, there's been a call for you from Mrs Katie Sorel. She needs to see you urgently. The duty officer told her he would give you her message as soon as you came in, but she sounded so desperate he had second thoughts and decided to phone you at once."

"Did she say why?" Tansey asked, with his mouth full.

"Only that she had heard from Oliver."

"From Oliver! Good! At least I hope it's good." Tansey ate rapidly.

"Dick, you must finish your breakfast properly."

"Yes, dear!" he mocked her.

But, ten minutes later, having kissed his wife and his small son goodbye for the day, Chief Inspector Tansey was on his way to Headquarters. Not long after that, having learnt no more from the duty officer concerning Katie's call, he and Sergeant Abbot were speeding towards Colombury. He told Abbot what he had achieved the previous day in Reading. Abbot was not particularly impressed, though he remarked that he had a suspicion that both Rowe's arms were tattooed.

"But I really can't imagine Vic Rowe calmly trying to sell the Widow's jewellery, sir," he said, "not just two days after he had killed her. It doesn't seem to me in character somehow. For that matter, I can't see him going upstairs and searching for the stuff and nicking it — and then joining a birthday party. We did check his alibi and it fitted. I think it more likely that if he had killed her he'd have been so horrified by what he'd done, that he'd have bolted immediately."

"I agree. He seems to be violent-tempered but not cold-blooded. However, he does fit Mr Grove's description, and there is that reference to a climbing rose. If you're right about his arms being tattooed — "

"Grove couldn't say what kind of tattoo, you told me, sir. A lot of men have tattoos of one type or another, not that I'd fancy one myself."

"Nor would I, Abbot, but I take your point. A lot of men do. I suppose they think it's macho."

"Vic Rowe hardly has to worry about that, sir. He's a tough character, all right."

★ ★ ★

Abbot dropped Tansey off at the end of the lane where Katie lived, and he went alone to her cottage. When she opened the door he thought she must be ill. Her face was drawn and grey, with dark circles under her eyes as if she hadn't slept the night before, and her skin was blotched from crying. She seized him by the arm and practically

227

pulled him into the front room.

"Oh, Chief Inspector, I'm so glad you've come."

But now that he was there she didn't seem to know what to say or do. She waved him to a chair and sat in front of her sewing-machine, as if its familiarity might give her courage. There was no sign of the little girl.

"Joy not here?" Tansey asked as an opening gambit.

"She's still in bed. She sleeps a lot."

Tansey didn't know whether to believe her or not. "Mrs Sorel," he said. "I understand you've heard from Oliver Vail. Did he telephone you?"

"No. He wrote to me."

Tansey was forced to prompt her. "When? It was too early for your post to have arrived when you phoned Headquarters this morning."

"Yesterday afternoon. The parcel came by a courier service, and this letter was inside. The man said he'd been instructed not to deliver it any earlier. There was a long letter in it. I didn't know what to do. I lay awake all night wondering if I should tell you. I love

Oliver, Chief Inspector. I wouldn't do anything to harm him, but it's better you should put him in prison than that he should kill himself, and I'm so afraid that's what he intends."

Katie drew a long, shuddering breath. "You'd better read the letter. Here it is." She took it from the pocket of her skirt and passed it to Tansey. "I'll go and make us some coffee, and see that Joy's all right."

In spite of his long experience, Tansey looked at the envelope that Katie had given him with some distaste. It had her name written on it in neat upright handwriting, and with a feeling of reluctance he withdrew from it two sheets of cheap notepaper. He knew, even before he read, 'My dearest darling,' that this was going to be a very private letter.

But it was more than that. It was businesslike, touchingly considerate and a confession that Oliver Vail had indeed killed his mother, though without making any effort to explain why. Tansey skimmed through it, and then read it again more slowly. Katie was taking her time with Joy, and he was glad not to be interrupted.

The address at the top of the letter was the Public Library, Reading. The date was the previous Thursday, the day after Lydia Vail had been killed. But even on second reading Tansey was impressed by the seeming calm of the writer. It would tell against him when the case came to court, he thought.

Oliver Vail had written:

My dearest darling, I am so terribly sorry to have caused you the sorrow and grief that I know I must have done, and there will be more to come. I love you deeply and truly, but we have no future. I used to dream of a house outside Colombury, with a garden where we would have had meals on the patio in the summer, and perhaps I could have put up a swing for Joy, a place where the three of us would be together and be happy. But it was not to come about.

I killed my mother. It was a dreadful thing to do, but I did it. I loved her, not as I love you, but I did love her, though she wasn't always easy to love. I promised my father when he knew he was going to die that I would always take care of her and I did my best to keep that promise. But her end is my end too.

After I had killed her my mind blacked out. I remember washing, not that there was much blood on me, and I fled. The Jag was there so I took it. I drove around. God knows where. I spent the night in the car. I'll spare you the details. Next day I came to my senses. I realized what I had done and what I would have to do, but before that I decided I would go down to the Isle of Wight for a few days. I had been so happy there as a child, as I've often told you, while my father was alive and well. Then suddenly everything changed. I suppose it was when they realized how ill he was, but they tried to shelter me from what was to come, and I didn't understand.

Darling, I must stop waffling and be practical. It's too easy to dwell on the past when there is no future. The money — fifteen thousand pounds — I'm sending you is from the sale of the Jaguar. Legally it's not mine, but that doesn't matter. Don't tell anyone. Just keep it. You should have it for the happiness you've given me, and otherwise it will only go to charity. I wish it could have been more.

Goodbye, my dearest one, and all my love. Take care of yourself.

Oliver.

PS. I saw the little xylophone in a toyshop and couldn't resist it. I hope Joy will like it. Do you remember how she loved that drum and how upset she was when it was destroyed? Better say you bought the xylophone yourself to avoid any similar trouble.

My love again, as always.

O.

The door opened and Katie came in. She was carrying two cups of coffee and a sugar-bowl on a small tray. Tansey shook his head at the sugar.

"I'll have to take the letter," he said, "and the money. I'll give you a receipt, of course. Did you keep the wrapping?"

"Yes. It's in the kitchen. You won't want the xylophone, will you? I haven't given it to Joy yet, but — "

"No. That won't be necessary. What happened to the drum that Oliver mentions?"

"My ex-husband broke it when he discovered it was a present from Oliver."

Tansey hesitated. It was not his business, but — "Mrs Sorel, if your ex-husband ever bothers you, you should go to the police."

"To Sergeant Donaldson?" Katie laughed. "Tom would take him apart. Chief Inspector, can I have my letter back later?"

"In due course, yes, if you mean the original. In the meantime, I'll make sure you get a photocopy. I don't know what will happen to the money."

"I don't care about the money, but I'd like the letter. Really all I want is for you to find Oliver before — before he kills himself. Now you know he's on the Isle of Wight it shouldn't be difficult, should it?"

"No indeed. We should find him in no time."

Tansey hadn't the heart to tell her that the police had been searching for Oliver Vail on the Isle of Wight for several days without any success, and he wondered if Oliver might not be already dead. He drank his coffee quickly and was glad to get out of the slightly claustrophobic atmosphere of Katie Sorel's cottage and rejoin Abbot.

"Message came through from Forensic, sir," Abbot said. "Blood and tissue on the clothes that dachshund dragged out of the rabbit hole correspond with Mrs Vail's."

"Good," said Tansey absentmindedly. "Any news on the Jaguar?"

"Not yet, sir."

"OK. Back to HQ, Abbot. Katie Sorel's just given me fifteen thousand pounds, sent to her by Oliver, and I'm not driving around with that in my pocket. Rowe will have to wait."

★ ★ ★

In the afternoon, after an early lunch, they set off once again for Little Chipping. Tansey decided to stop at the vicarage, where Basil Moore opened the front door to them.

"Come in, Chief Inspector, Sergeant. Have you any news of Oliver yet?"

"Nothing definite, sir, but I think the pieces are beginning to fit together. We've found the Jaguar and some of Mrs Vail's jewellery. However, that's for your private information."

"Right. Let's go into my study. I suppose this isn't a social call?"

"No, Vicar. We have some questions. They may seem rather odd, but they do have a purpose." And when they were settled, "First, I want to ask you about tattoos."

"Tattoos?" Basil Moore laughed. "That certainly is odd! I'd never have guessed. I'm afraid I know nothing about them."

"But you know a lot of people in the neighbourhood, and if you don't mind my saying so, I'm sure you're observant."

"Thank you, Chief Inspector, and also as a vicar someone to be trusted, I hope."

Tansey grinned his acknowledgement. "We're trying to trace a man who has a tattoo on his lower arm. Can you think of anyone from Little Chipping and around who fits that description?"

"Several. Vic Rowe, for one. He has a rose on each wrist — a symbol of his profession, I suppose. Then there's Fred Denham, Meg's husband. Oh, and Sidney Corbet who runs our pub. He used to be a seaman once. You know, Chief Inspector, any non-officer who was ever in the Navy, Royal or Merchant, is likely to have a tattoo. Haven't you got any more to go on?"

"A little," Tansey said.

But he didn't volunteer it. He was thinking there was no longer National Service and not many young men from the Cotswolds, in the centre of England, would choose to go to sea, and he wondered if he was wasting his time. Since it was not Oliver Vail who had sold the jewellery, and Oliver had admitted killing his mother, did it matter who had been in Mr Grove's shop in Reading the previous Friday morning?

"Sir," Abbot interrupted his thoughts.

"Katie Sorel's ex-husband, Tom, is a merchant seaman."

"Yes. I had remembered, but he doesn't fit Grove's description, does he? He'd got fair hair and a rather thin face."

"I was just thinking about him being a seaman. I've no idea if he's got a tattoo or not, but I suppose we can rule him out — and Mr Corbet. He'd have been behind his bar on Friday morning."

"Yes. I can vouch for Sidney Corbet if he needs an alibi for Friday morning and so can lots of others," said Basil Moore unexpectedly. "He was in his pub all right."

"We had no suspicions of him, Vicar, I assure you," Tansey said. "Now we can forget tattoos and consider ties — or, to be more exact, one particular tie, dark blue with red spots."

"There must be a lot of those around, too," Moore said.

"Yes, but not draped over a rhododendron near the Vails' back door on Wednesday evening last. I must ask you, sir, did you see it on Thursday morning when you and Mr Corbet arrived."

"No, *I* didn't see it then, and Sidney never mentioned it. Of course we might not have noticed it. We were intent on getting into the house and finding Mrs Vail."

"Of course," Tansey said and asked himself if there had been a certain evasiveness in Moore's reply, or if he had imagined it. "I'll have to ask Meg Denham. She was the first, as far as we know, to arrive at the scene on Thursday morning. There was no milk delivery there on Thursdays, we gather."

"Actually it's one of Meg's days for the Vails, but as she couldn't go there today, my wife suggested she might help clear out our attics. They need doing and she needs the money. I'll fetch her."

"I'll do it, sir," Abbot volunteered, catching a warning glance from Tansey.

For a big man Abbot was quick on his feet. He beat the vicar to the door and, running up the stairs to the first floor, called to Mrs Denham. She came down a further flight of stairs at once and, surprised to see Abbot, apologized for her appearance. She was wearing an overall and slippers and her hair was tied up in an old scarf. Her face and hands were smeared with dust. She apologized again to the Chief Inspector.

"That's all right, Mrs Denham," Tansey said. "I'm sorry to interrupt your work. But just one question. When you went to the Vails' house on Thursday morning, did you see a dark blue tie with red spots draped over a bush?"

"No! I never seen no tie!" she replied vehemently, staring Tansey straight in the face.

"Are you sure, Meg?" Basil Moore asked, surprised at her reaction. "It could be important."

"I said no and I meant no!" She glared at each of the three men in turn, and it was obvious she was lying. Normally she wouldn't have dreamt of addressing the vicar so rudely. "If that's all I'll get back to Mrs Moore."

"Yes, that's all, Meg," said Moore after a nod from Tansey.

But when Meg had gone Tansey said, "Perhaps you could persuade her to tell us the truth, sir. It's not a good idea to lie to the police."

"I'll speak to her," the vicar said.

★ ★ ★

If the call at the vicarage was unsatisfactory, so were the other calls Tansey and Abbot made in Little Chipping. Sidney Corbet supported the vicar, but he was more positive; he hadn't seen a tie of any kind on a bush or anywhere else. Fred Denham, whom they found cleaning out the gutters of his cottage, his sleeves rolled up to reveal intricate tattoos on both his lower arms, said he had spent Friday morning at home answering a job vacancy he had seen in the previous day's *Courier*. And Vic Rowe claimed to have been working at Major Tomlinson's house all day Friday, but the Tomlinsons were away on holiday, so he had no alibi.

"Well, that was a waste of an afternoon, Abbot," Tansey said as they drove back to Kidlington.

He was wrong. He had been given a lead which he had ignored, and the results would prove disastrous.

15

ELAINE PULMAN'S body was found early next morning by a couple of hikers.

They were students from the north of England having a cheap holiday. They had spent the previous night camping in a field — they carried their own tent with them — and were on their way to Colombury to have breakfast and inquire about trains home. Cross-questioned first by Sergeant Donaldson, then by Inspector Whitelaw, and later by Chief Inspector Tansey, they denied ever having heard of Mrs Lydia Vail or Oliver Vail or Elaine Pulman, and claimed that Little Chipping was just a name on a map as far as they were concerned. They admitted to carrying a radio, but said they only used it to listen to pop music when they stopped for a meal or were settling down for the night, and they didn't buy newspapers.

The girl became indignant at the many

questions, and insisted on telephoning her father who, she assured Tansey, was an eminent lawyer and knew how to deal with stupid policemen. It turned out, however, that she had maligned her parent. His sympathy was all with the Chief Inspector and he told his daughter in no uncertain terms to do whatever she was told.

"So let's start again," Tansey said when she had placated her father and put down the receiver. "I don't believe that either of you is implicated in the murder, but your evidence is needed. Please try to be helpful. The sooner you both make a clear statement which you can sign, the sooner you can go."

They hadn't known exactly where they were, but they had seen what was clearly a well-worn track across a field and they guessed that it led in the general direction of Colombury. In fact, it was the path that led from Little Chipping to the market town. They had gone some distance when the girl had noticed what looked like a bundle of clothes half in and half out of a ditch. The boy had gone to see what it was.

"No, I never touched it," he said and shivered. "It was revolting. It made me vomit. I'd not seen a dead person before."

"He wouldn't let me look," the girl said. "We hurried on to Colombury and asked the way to the police station, and we've been here all the morning."

"It was revolting," the boy repeated, remembering what he had seen. "Disgusting."

★ ★ ★

Tansey, who had watched Dr Ghent examine the body *in situ*, understood the young man's feelings. Elaine Pulman, who when alive had been an attractive and vivacious woman, was not a pretty sight in death. She had been strangled. There was a silk scarf tied tight around her neck, her face was discoloured and her tongue lolled out of the side of her mouth. In addition, she was naked from the waist down. Her skirt had been rucked up and her undergarments, torn and broken, suggesting they had been pulled off with some violence, had been thrown into the ditch, together with her shoes and shoulder-bag. There had been no attempt to hide the body.

"Death by strangulation?" he asked Ghent.

"It would seem so," said the pathologist with his usual reluctance to commit himself to any statement until he had performed the autopsy.

"Has she been raped?"

"She'd certainly had intercourse fairly recently. There's dried semen on her thighs, but no obvious signs of forcible entry. Of course, she could have been killed first. It has been known, especially if the killer is a rejected lover. I can't tell you any more until I've done the PM."

"Not a nice idea," said Tansey, and thought of Vic Rowe. "What about time? Can you give us a clue?"

Dr Ghent shrugged. "It was a warm night. At a guess I'd say around midnight. And if you'd like another guess I'd say the attack took place close by, and she was dragged into the ditch afterwards. She was a big girl, and she wouldn't have been easy to carry when dead."

"Thanks," said Tansey, who had

already worked this out for himself but didn't want to discourage any voluntary comments from Ghent. "Unfortunately this rough grass is unlikely to provide any evidence, but we'll have to see. I'll have a word with Inspector Whitelaw." The Inspector, having driven the Incident Van and its team over from the Vails', was organizing a cordon around the area and tarpaulins to cover the site. "He'll arrange for a fingertip search."

★ ★ ★

"To Little Chipping and the Ploughman's, Abbot," said Tansey, getting into the car and fastening his seat belt. "We'll have to break the news to the Corbets, and we need to learn what they can tell us about Elaine's movements yesterday evening."

"Yes, sir." Abbot sighed. "This used to be such a peaceful place," he said as he drove off, "and now two separate murders in the district in a week. It's unbelievable."

"If they *are* separate murders."

"Sir, you can't believe that Oliver Vail

245

had anything to do with Elaine's death. He's in the Isle of Wight."

"He was. He may not still be there. But to answer your question, no, Abbot, I don't believe Oliver Vail was personally responsible for Elaine's death. However, either we have to predicate a completely separate murder, which you yourself said was unbelievable, or look for some connection between them — and already we've got Elaine herself as a ready-made connection. Frankly I don't know. This killing, happening just now, seems an odd coincidence to me, and I don't like coincidences."

"There are such things, sir." Abbot was tentative.

"Of course there are," Tansey agreed, "but it does no harm to suspect them."

Abbot didn't argue. He sometimes found the Chief Inspector's thought processes impenetrable, and when this happened it was best to accept what he was told without question. He concentrated on his driving, not that he had any desire to reach the Ploughman's Arms. He was sure the Corbets were going to take Elaine's death hard, and he was thankful that it would be Tansey's job to break the news to them.

In fact, the Corbets had already heard about the tragedy. Sergeant Donaldson had informed them. Rose was in tears and Sidney was trying to hide his grief in a show of anger. Striding up and down the bar, he looked as if he would be prepared to wreck his own pub.

"I could kill the bastard who did it," he said. "She was a good girl, a sweet, kind girl. Oh, I know, people gossiped about her, said she was a tart and led men on, but that wasn't our Elaine. She was almost like a daughter to us. She'd had one hell of a life when she was young and . . . "

Tansey let him talk. It would have been difficult to stop him, and anyhow they were learning about Elaine Pulman. As a child she had been put in care, but her foster father had been a drunk who had abused her and maltreated her. She had run away. From the age of fifteen she had somehow managed to survive until eight years ago she had turned up at the Ploughman's in answer to an advertisement Sidney had put in

247

the *Courier*. She had no experience, no references and she admitted to being homeless, but they had taken her on.

"And never regretted it," Sidney Corbet said stoutly. "It was one of the best things we ever did."

"We're going to miss her so much," added Rose, her voice thick with tears. "I can't really believe she's dead. Chief Inspector, is it true she was raped?"

"Who told you that?"

"Sergeant Donaldson. When we found she hadn't come home last night we were worried, and Sidney phoned around her friends. But no one knew where she was, so eventually we tried the police station in case she had had an accident. And Donaldson told us she had been raped and then strangled."

"He had no right," said Tansey, controlling his anger and promising himself that Donaldson would pay for his callousness. "Absolutely no right, and it may well not be true. She's dead, yes. Her body was found in a field by two young students and her clothes were torn, but that's all we know so far."

"I only hope she didn't suffer much," Rose said.

"Where's she been taken?" Sidney asked. "She had no next-of-kin, but Rose and I will be responsible. She'll be buried here in Little Chipping."

"Mr Corbet, that may not be possible for a while," Tansey warned. "She's been taken to Oxford. There'll have to be a post-mortem and an inquest."

"And you've got to catch the bugger who did it."

"Yes," said Tansey flatly, "and you may be able to help us. Elaine went into Colombury yesterday evening. To meet friends?"

"Yes, Tuesday's one of our slacker nights and there was a movie she wanted to see. She'd arranged to go with Monica Carter, but — "

"Monica Carter?" Abbot queried, looking up from his notebook.

"She lives with her parents in one of the council houses on the outskirts of Colombury, and she works in Watson's flower shop. She's younger than Elaine, but they are — were — good friends."

"Thank you," Abbot murmured.

"Elaine said she was hoping to persuade Katie Sorel to go with them, if old Mrs Sorel would babysit for Joy, because she thought it would be good for Katie to be taken out of herself, and forget about Oliver for a while."

"And Katie did go with them," Rose broke in. "Sidney phoned her this morning. She said she and Monica were worried about Elaine walking back to Little Chipping across the fields alone, but Elaine had often done it before. She had no fears, and it was a lovely night with a full moon."

Rose began to cry again, and Sidney Corbet looked appealingly at Tansey. "We'll have to open up soon. Elaine would want it, apart from the law. If it's all right with you, Chief Inspector, I'll phone young Alan Moore. He likes to help out here occasionally, though whether he'll want to today I don't know. He was very fond of Elaine. Anyway, I'll have to call the vicar. The whole village is going to miss her, not only us," he ended sadly.

★ ★ ★

250

When the two detectives came out of the Ploughman's they saw Miss Mary Gore sweeping her front path. They would have ignored her, but she waved her broom at them.

"Old witch," Abbot muttered.

"We'd better see what she wants."

What Miss Gore wanted was to know if it was true that Elaine Pulman had been found dead in a ditch. She had heard this item of gossip from Mrs Carter who ran the village store; Mrs Carter's sister-in-law, mother of Monica who had been to the cinema with Elaine the previous evening, had telephoned the news, including the fact that Monica was devastated.

"Mind you, I'm not in the least surprised," Miss Gore said when Tansey confirmed what she had heard. "That girl had it coming to her. She only got what she deserved."

Tansey couldn't hide his distaste. "It's lucky we don't all get what we deserve, Miss Gore. Now, are you going to invite us into your house, or shall we continue this interview at the police station?"

She stared at him. "What do you mean?"

"What I said, Miss Gore. I think you may know more about Miss Pulman than we do, and we'd like to know what it is. I must remind you that it's an offence to withhold evidence from the police, most especially when they are investigating not one, but two cases of murder."

There was an appreciable pause. Then she said, "Very well. Come along in."

She led them into her front room, which was excessively tidy, though cluttered with small tables and ornaments. The chairs looked, and were, uncomfortable. Abbot, who had been directed to a particularly straight-backed hard seat, had his revenge by taking out his notebook ostentatiously, ready to record anything that was said. He was rewarded by a reproachful glare from Miss Gore, before she turned her attention to Tansey.

"You want to know why I made that remark about Elaine Pulman, Chief Inspector? I'll tell you. The girl was no better than a prostitute. Oh, I'm not saying she did it for money, but she was always after men. My sister and I were

252

walking in the woods one day when we went a little off the path and practically fell over Elaine and that man Vic Rowe in a small clearing, shamefully having intercourse. In a public place! Disgusting, I call it."

"I believe they were engaged at one time."

Mary Gore sniffed. "That's no excuse. I've seen her playing up to Oliver Vail — not that she got very far with him — and making up to that Moore boy, who's scarcely more than a child. The vicar should look out for him."

"Is that all, Miss Gore?" Tansey asked. "For your information Miss Pulman was walking home from Colombury alone yesterday evening when she was assaulted. She had been to the cinema with two young *women* friends."

"In the hope of picking up some young male friends, I'll be bound." Miss Gore had her prejudices, and nothing would shake them. "And that is *not* all, Chief Inspector. She wasn't above trying to break up marriages, and I'm not referring to the Corbets, though if I were Rose Corbet I wouldn't have given the girl houseroom. No, I'm talking about the Smiths, that nice couple who were staying with me last week."

"Ah yes," said Tansey as Mary Gore paused for breath. "Mr and *Mrs* Smith."

Miss Gore, who was accustomed to underlining her own words metaphorically, ignored Tansey's emphasis on 'Mrs'. "The day before the Smiths left — suddenly, because they were unhappy and wanted to go home; I'll tell you why — Elaine took Paul Smith up into the woods behind the Vails' house and don't ask me what went on, but he was fifteen to twenty minutes late for his evening meal, and when he came in his shirt wasn't buttoned properly and there was lipstick on his face."

"How do you know all this, Miss Gore?"

"I saw him when he came in, of course, and told him I'd kept his meal hot for him. Then later I overheard them quarrelling — Mr and Mrs Smith, I mean. I couldn't help it. They were literally shouting at each other. And I heard him admit he'd been in the woods with Elaine. Just walking, he said, as if anyone would believe that, him being in the state he was."

Mary Gore stopped speaking and regarded Tansey in triumph. Sensing that she had finished spewing out her venom and they would learn no more from her, Tansey stood up. It took an effort to thank her and say goodbye politely. Both he and Abbot were glad to get out of the house into the clean summer air.

* * *

If Abbot expected the Chief Inspector to make some caustic remark about Miss Mary Gore he was disappointed. Tansey merely told him to ask at the garage which was Vic Rowe's house.

"I will, sir, but Rowe won't be home now."

"No, but some of the family may, and perhaps they may be among the two or three people in this place who haven't heard about Elaine yet. I think someone said that Rowe lived with his brother and sister-in-law."

This proved to be right. Mrs Rowe, a

woman in her early thirties, came to the door, a toddler hanging on to her skirt. There was the sound of another child crying in the background. She wiped her hands on her apron and regarded the two police officers with irritation, making it clear that they had interrupted some vital domestic process.

"I'm Chief Inspector — " Tansey began.

"I know who you are. Everyone in the village knows." It wasn't an auspicious start, and she continued, "If you want to see Vic, you can't."

"Is he here?"

"Yes, he's here — in bed. He's got that bug what's going about, and he's really sick — poor lamb."

At least someone's fond of him, Tansey thought, and said, "I'm sorry to hear that. When was Mr Rowe taken ill?"

"Yesterday. Luckily it was his day for working at Dr Maitland's and the doctor and his wife, who are kind folk, brought him home soon after midday. Dr Maitland gave him some pills and said he'd pop in later this morning to see how Vic was, for which I'm grateful because his temperature's still over a hundred. And I've a sick child too. Up half the night I was; believe me, between them I've got my hands full."

"Yes, of course, Mrs Rowe. We're sorry to have disturbed you. We hope your invalids will be better soon."

Placated, she asked, "Why did you want Vic?"

"Nothing important," Tansey lied. "Just to ask him if he'd seen anyone, apart from Mrs Vail, near her house when he left last Wednesday. It can wait."

★ ★ ★

"Do you know this Dr Maitland, Abbot?" Tansey said as once more they returned to their car.

"Yes, sir. He's been practising here for years. He's more or less retired now, takes no new patients, but he's a fine doctor."

"We'll have to check with him, needless to say, but it looks as if this bug has given Vic Rowe an excellent alibi."

"It certainly does. Who would have thought that anyone would be grateful for a bug?" Abbot said, grinning.

16

WHY? Tansey asked himself. Why Elaine? Her handbag had been rifled, and there was the remote possibility that she had been killed by some casual vagrant, a hopeful thief, as had been considered in the case of Lydia Vail. There was also the possibility that her rape, if she had been raped, and her death had been the work of a local man whose advances she had turned down as had been suggested earlier; even if this were so, the murderer could not have been Vic Rowe, for Dr Maitland had given him a firm alibi. Finally, there was the possibility that she had had to be silenced; perhaps, without having been aware of it, she had known something about Mrs Vail's death which her killer didn't want to become public — but, on the other hand, Oliver Vail had already admitted responsibility for his mother's death. Nevertheless . . .

Elaine's friends, Monica Carter and

Katie Sorel, had been questioned separately and their stories had coincided. Elaine had picked up Monica at her council house on the outskirts of Colombury, and together they had gone to persuade Katie to join them. At first she had been reluctant, but eventually she had agreed to come, if old Mrs Sorel would be prepared to babysit for Joy. When this had been arranged, the three women had gone to the cinema.

The film had lasted longer than they had expected. Afterwards they had gone to have a drink at the Windrush Arms, but Tom Sorel had been there and they hadn't lingered. Anyway, it was getting late. Katie was anxious to get home to Joy, and Monica knew that her mother wouldn't go to bed until her daughter had come in. Both Katie and Monica expressed doubts about Elaine walking back to Little Chipping alone, but it was a bright moonlit night and she had often done it before. Besides, there was no option. Elaine absolutely refused to ask if anyone in the Windrush Arms was going her way and would give her a lift.

"She said it would be an open invitation to trouble," Katie had remarked sadly, "but if only we'd known. I can't really believe it," she had added. "Elaine was such a nice, kind, outgoing girl. She ought not to have died like that, just by chance, as if her death was something casual and unimportant."

But had it been by chance, Tansey wondered. The scarf with which Elaine Pulman had been strangled puzzled him. According to Forensic, it was an inexpensive scarf that could have been bought in any store, with nothing to distinguish it, but it had a pattern of white flowers on a green background and was a most unlikely scarf for any man to have worn. And both Katie and Monica had been adamant; Elaine had not been wearing a scarf the previous evening and, if she had been, it would not have been green for she was superstitious and believed that green was her unlucky colour.

Tansey could think of only one reasonable explanation. Elaine Pulman's murder had been premeditated. That probably meant that she had known something. But what? What had she seen? According to Miss Mary Gore, Elaine had been in the woods with Paul Smith about the time that Lydia Vail had been murdered. Was this significant? And who had known about the expedition to the cinema and the opportunity this might offer?

Tansey brought his report up to date on what had become for him the Vail/Pulman case. He looked at his watch; all he had to do was make sure the document was photocopied and placed in the in-trays of the Chief Constable and other senior officers concerned, for their perusal in the morning. Then he could pack up and go home, for once reasonably early.

He pushed back his chair and made to get up, but changed his mind and reached for the phone. Paul Smith answered on the second ring as if he had been expecting a call. He agreed reluctantly that he would be in for the next hour and would wait for the Chief Inspector.

★ ★ ★

Paul Smith had a basement flat in a house in Oxford near the railway station. It was clean but gloomy, and already on this pleasant summer evening he had been forced to put on the light, which didn't flatter the shabby furniture or the threadbare carpet. However, the room was saved from being miserable by the presence of a sophisticated word processor on the desk, and the books in shelves on most of the wall space, and scattered everywhere.

Smith waved Tansey to an armchair, which was battered but surprisingly comfortable, and Tansey thought that he preferred these surroundings to Miss Gore's front room with its innumerable little tables and clutter of small ornaments.

"Well, Chief Inspector, what can I do for you?" Smith asked, deliberately looking at his watch, as if to imply that his time was precious and that he had another engagement. "I've told you all I know about Little Chipping and its inhabitants. Personally I never want to see the place again. It was not a good holiday."

"I still believe there are one or two

more points you can clarify — points that were overlooked at our last meeting — but first I'd like to know what you were doing yesterday evening."

"Yesterday evening." Smith stared at him. "Why?"

"Perhaps you'd answer my question."

Smith hesitated, then decided to acquiesce with fair grace. "Certainly," he said. "I had dinner with my former tutor who's a good friend of mine. He has rooms in Christ Church where we retired after a lengthy meal, and we chatted until the small hours. He's been in the States for the last year, and we had a lot of catching up to do. Then I walked back home." He paused, and added, "I'm sure he'll answer for me if it's necessary, and I assure you he's a reputable witness. Incidentally, several other people dropped in during the evening, so you could ask them too if you really think it worth while. I'll give you their names."

"Thank you," said Tansey, ignoring Smith's sarcasm.

"Now, will you do me the courtesy of telling me why I need an alibi for yesterday evening, which it seems I do?"

"Yesterday evening, sometime around midnight, Elaine Pulman was killed."

"Killed? You mean murdered? Oh no! How?" Smith regarded Tansey with horror but, as he absorbed what he had been told, his expression became one of anxious anger. "And you've come to see *me* to ask *me* for an alibi? Why me? For God's sake, I scarcely knew the woman."

"You're jumping to conclusions, Mr Smith. That is not why I've come to see you," Tansey said calmly, "though it does no harm to check that you're in the clear, does it?"

"Like hell it does! You've no right — "

"I've every right, Mr Smith. Last night, around midnight as I say, Elaine Pulman was murdered, probably after being raped. This is the second violent death in a small community within a week. I'm sure you don't want there to be a third, any more than I do. So I appeal for your help."

"How on earth can I help? It's true what I said. I scarcely knew her. She was just the girl who served drinks in the village pub."

"I'll explain." Tansey saw no reason to spare Smith's feelings. "Although the methods of murder in the two cases were dissimilar — Elaine Pulman was strangled with a scarf either before or after the probable rape — there is a strong possibility that they are connected. The reason for killing Elaine may have been that when she was in the woods behind the Vails' house on the evening that Lydia Vail was killed, she saw or heard something which later she connected with the killer, and he — "

"But I thought that Oliver Vail — "

"Ah, there you go, jumping to conclusions again, Mr Smith." If Abbot had been with them, Tansey thought, he would at this point have given his little cough, warning the Chief Inspector that he was being too tough with this witness. "Now, I gather you were with Elaine Pulman in the woods that Wednesday evening. Is that so?" he continued more gently.

"We went for a walk," Smith admitted.

"You just told me you hardly knew her. Was it a date? Where did you go? What did you do?"

Smith flushed. "Well — I — we — Look, is this relevent?"

Tansey relented. "I think you've said enough. Anyway, you were so occupied that you forgot the time. Suddenly it was six-thirty, when you should have been back for your evening meal at Miss Gore's establishment — and we know how strict she is. But Elaine pointed out that you could cut across the Vails' property which would save several minutes. Am I right?"

"Yes." Smith nodded.

"Now, this is what I want to know, Mr Smith. Please think carefully. Did you or Elaine see anyone — man, woman or child — when you were about to leave the woods?"

"Only Oliver Vail."

"You're positive it was Oliver Vail? You'd swear to it?"

"No, I couldn't; I didn't know him. But Elaine said it was Vail."

"Just after six-thirty?" Tansey queried, thinking that someone was not telling the truth.

"Probably nearer six-forty. Say thirty-five. But I can't be accurate to the minute."

"Of course not. You're doing quite well, Mr Smith. Was Vail approaching or leaving the house?"

"Leaving — or that was the impression I got. He could have been merely going to the garage, I suppose. I ran as soon as I was sure he was out of sight."

"Did you see the Vails' car? It's a Jaguar."

"No. I didn't see any car, but I — I think I heard one driving away." Smith shook his head in exasperation. "I'm damned if I can remember whether that was before or after we saw Vail. Sorry."

"That's all right, Mr Smith. Can you describe the man you saw?"

"Chief Inspector!" Smith protested. "We didn't see him for more than a minute. In fact, Elaine thought he was someone else at first. But my impression was that he was tall and fair."

"Elaine thought he might be someone else?" Tansey kept his voice steady, but he felt excitement rising in him. "What exactly did she say?"

"She said, 'Hang on a moment, Paul, there's someone by the house. It looks like — no, it can't be. He's not home.

It's Oliver!' As far as I can recall, Chief Inspector, she was then quite sure it was Oliver."

Tansey's momentary excitement subsided, but he was schooled in hiding disappointment. "OK, Mr Smith. Elaine said the man you both saw was Oliver Vail. She didn't mention the other chap's name — the man who wasn't at home — the character she thought might have been Oliver?"

"No! Definitely not!"

"Well, let's go on. What about his clothes? You must have got some impression."

Smith looked at Tansey curiously. "I suppose this is important. Is it?"

Tansey shrugged. "It could be, but don't worry about that. Do your best to remember."

"I think he was wearing slacks — light grey or blue — and a blouson. I think the blouson was navy blue, but it could have been black. I suppose my general impression as I visualize it is that he was basically dressed in blue, the blouson a lot darker than the trousers."

"He was definitely not wearing a — a

business suit?" Tansey had nearly called it a 'banking suit', like Jan Moore.

"Oh no! He looked smart enough, but casual — at least from a distance. Chief Inspector, I must stress I only caught a glimpse of the man, and I had other things on my mind. If I had known there was going to be an observation test I would have concentrated more."

"Of course."

The two men were no longer antagonistic. Smith, thankful that his sex life was not to be questioned further, had stopped being aggressive. For his part Tansey was pleased with Smith's efforts at cooperation.

"I only hope I've been of some use, Chief Inspector." Paul Smith spoke sincerely. "I never met the Widow, as everyone seemed to call her, but Elaine was a nice girl. I'm truly sorry about her death, and if anything I've told you will help to unravel the puzzle, though I can't imagine how it could, I'll be glad."

"Mr Smith, one never knows when one small piece of information may form a keystone in a case, so I'm grateful for

270

your time," Tansey said acknowledging Smith's remarks.

But, driving home, he thought that instead of helping to unravel any puzzle, Smith had complicated it. The pieces simply did not fit together.

17

"IT simply does not add up, sir," Tansey said.

He was in the office of the Chief Constable, Philip Midvale, discussing with him the murders of Lydia Vail and Elaine Pulman. Midvale had already read Tansey's reports, and had seen for himself the difficulties inherent in the case or, if they were not connected, the two separate cases.

"If only Oliver Vail hadn't made that voluntary confession," Tansey said. He added to himself, "And if only we could manage to find him."

"His confession certainly doesn't make things any simpler," Midvale agreed. He shifted in the chair which had been specially made to accommodate his bulk, and thought that if his arthritis got much worse he would have to contemplate resignation. "Of course, as you know perfectly well, individuals do sometimes confess to murders they haven't committed, even without any police pressure. Has it occurred to you, Chief Inspector, that Vail might have returned home determined to face up to his mother? His girlfriend — what's her name? — Katie Sorel admits she had given him an ultimatum; he had to choose between her and his ma for she was tired of waiting. However, Vail finds his mother's dead, brutally murdered and, overcome with remorse that he was going to leave her, has a brainstorm of some kind and convinces himself that *he* killed her."

"Not precisely in those terms, sir," Tansey said warily. The Chief Constable would sometimes produce scenarios which he knew were weak, and would then wait to see what valid criticism the officer he was addressing would produce in reply; but on other occasions he was in earnest and then he didn't like to be flatly contradicted.

Tansey went on, "I had considered the possibility of Vail having a brainstorm, but rather as a precursor to killing his mother, perhaps after a violent argument, than as a result of finding her dead."

The Chief Constable nodded as he glanced through the reports on the desk to refresh his memory. "Then there are all these times your witnesses quote. They worry me. The Vails' place seems to have been a hive of activity between about six o'clock and seven that Wednesday evening, and the times can't all be right. If Smith and Pulman saw Oliver Vail by the house at approximately six thirty-five, he was presumably inside the place when Thane, the poulterer bringing the duck from Oxford, heard water running. But where on earth was the Jaguar? No one admits to seeing it except Janice Moore who says it was there at about six forty-five, though she hadn't seen it arrive."

"Sir, Vail could have arrived home — but not before six-fifteen. He didn't leave Field's garage in Colombury till about six. He could have garaged the car, not expecting to need it, killed his mother, washed, changed into casual clothes, and was getting the Jaguar out of the garage again, which was when Smith and Elaine Pulman saw him. But he'd have needed to be extremely quick to achieve all that in twenty minutes."

"Impossibly quick, I would say. Moreover, the time is even tighter if the water Thane heard running was Oliver washing after the murder. And remember that whoever killed Lydia Vail struggled with her first. That would have used up a few minutes. Then he'd have had to go upstairs and get the rifle."

"I agree, sir. I can't believe it was all possible in the time. Besides, if Jan Moore's to be believed he had changed into a business suit by ten past seven, when he apparently drove off. You recall that Janice wasn't certain whether he was carrying a bag of any kind."

"So, Chief Inspector, at least we've proved that Elaine Pulman was wrong," said Midvale with satisfaction. "It was not Oliver Vail whom she saw. Therefore, we must ask ourselves who it was. We need to find him."

While Tansey silently reflected that this was a pretty obvious comment, Midvale made a great effort and pushed himself out of his chair to stand up. "This man could be a very important witness, or not impossibly the murderer, because if he was an innocent like Mr Thane why hasn't he come forward? Think about it, Tansey."

"Yes, sir."

Tansey hadn't needed the instruction. He had been thinking about this and many other points for some while, but thinking hadn't got him very far. Now he realized that the Chief Constable had no more to say on the subject either, no advice to give, no suggestions to make and, short of questioning everyone concerned yet again, he himself could think of nothing to do.

The case seemed to have reached an impasse, though there were always the oddities to consider, the tie on the rhododendron, the scarf with which Elaine had been strangled. For no apparent reason Dick Tansey suddenly felt more cheerful. Perhaps the Chief Constable had pointed him in a new direction after all.

★ ★ ★

As soon as he had returned to his own office the Chief Inspector put through a telephone call to the Reverend Basil

276

Moore. While he waited for someone at the vicarage to answer he thought of the report that had just arrived from Forensic; the Jaguar, though clean to the naked eye, had given up a number of secrets — hairs, sweat, fingerprints, but no blood or tissue — and yet Oliver Vail had supposedly driven the car immediately after he had killed his mother, almost certainly carrying at least a plastic shopping bag full of bloodstained garments. It was feasible, Tansey supposed.

"Hello! Hello! Basil Moore here. Hello!"

"Chief Inspector Tansey. Sorry, Vicar. I was distracted."

"I'm not surprised. You must have a lot on your mind at present. Mrs Vail's death was bad enough, but poor Elaine is going to leave a real gap in the village, and it's frightening too. People are beginning to ask who will be the next."

"I hope to God there won't be a next." Tansey's remark was heartfelt. "Vicar, what I wanted to ask is, have you had a word with Meg Denham about the tie she denied seeing?"

"Yes, but I regret to say that I wasn't very successful. Eventually she admitted she had seen the tie on the rhododendron bush and had been tempted to take it. But somehow I wasn't convinced. Meg's an honest woman. She's not a natural liar. And I'm pretty sure she was hiding something."

"Have you any idea what it might be, Vicar?"

"I have an idea, but it's merely an idea. Is this tie really important?"

"I don't know. It could be. At the moment I'm grateful for any scrap of information."

"All right, Chief Inspector."

There was a pause while Moore seemed to come to a decision. Then he said, "You understand I don't like to point a finger at anyone, but when I collected Meg's bag from the Vails' kitchen a tie fell out. I know it was an ordinary tie, but I had the impression I'd seen it before. I associated it with church on Sundays, and I wondered if it could be Oliver's. When you started asking questions about a tie, and Meg denied seeing one, the penny suddenly dropped.

I believe, though I could easily be wrong, that the tie belongs to Meg's husband, Fred, which would explain why she has been behaving so out of character."

"Fred Denham?" Tansey mused. "Would he have had any reason to go to the Vails' house?"

"It's conceivable. He's a skilled painter and decorator, but he's been out of work for a couple of years since the firm he worked for in Colombury went bust. He does casual jobs, but it would have been strange for Mrs Vail to employ him. In fact, she wasn't keen on employing any local labour at all. Still, Chief Inspector, for such as it's worth that's what occurred to me. The tie could be Fred Denham's; Meg recognized it, took it from the bush and put it in her bag."

"What kind of man is Denham?"

"A mild chap, bitter about being unemployed for so long, and ashamed that Meg has had to work so hard to make up for his inadequacy and keep the family together. I certainly can't imagine him killing Mrs Vail."

"And leaving his tie behind? It seems a bizarre thing to do. Nevertheless, I'll have to speak to him. Many thanks for your help, Vicar."

"I'm afraid it's more a duty than a pleasure on this occasion, Chief Inspector. I just hope Fred can produce a reasonable explanation."

I just hope he can produce some useful information, Tansey thought.

★ ★ ★

Tansey had scarcely replaced the receiver when Inspector Whitelaw came into the office. A man had phoned. He had demanded to speak to the Chief Inspector, and would accept no one else. He had refused to give his name or telephone number, but he had assured Whitelaw that it was important, and he would call again at noon.

"You spoke to him yourself? What was your impression?"

"He was authoritative, sir. Not a young man. I don't think it was a hoax call. To me he sounded genuine, but he could be a crank — someone who for one reason or another believed he needed to speak to you personally."

"And he gave you no idea what his business might be?"

"None."

"You'd advise that I speak to him?"

"I would, sir. There's a chance his reason for calling is connected with the Little Chipping murders. After all, you've had a fair amount of publicity recently because of them."

"Yes. It's a mistake to get one's name in the news. Noon, you said? I had been hoping to have a talk with Fred Denham. Ah well, that'll have to wait." Tansey was resigned. "This way at least I'll get some paperwork done."

★ ★ ★

The Chief Inspector was reading Dr Ghent's report on the post-mortem he had performed on Elaine Pulman when his phone rang at one minute past twelve. The report held nothing unexpected, and he put it aside with relief.

"Your call, Chief Inspector."

"Thank you." He waited a moment for the connection to be made, and said, "This is Detective Chief Inspector

281

Tansey. I gather you wished to speak to me."

"Yes. I would very much like to have a talk with you — in private. The telephone is not satisfactory, and I was hoping we might meet."

It was a pleasant voice, and Whitelaw had described it well, but Tansey was wary. "I'm a busy man," he said. "I would have to have an idea what your business with me was before I arranged a meeting."

"Of course. I understand. However, when I tell you who I am, the matter and the need for privacy will become clear. Chief Inspector, my name is Vail."

"Vail?" Tansey repeated stupidly, disbelieving that he could be speaking to Oliver Vail. "Not — not — "

"Oh no! My first name is Lionel. I'm a retired chartered accountant. My family and I live in Peebles, in Scotland."

"Are you related to Oliver?" Tansey was tentative.

"Father and son. You wouldn't doubt it if you saw us together, not that I've seen him or Lydia, my first wife, for at least ten years, but I suspect that since he's become a man, we're more alike than ever."

"I understood that his father — that you — "

There was a dismissive laugh on the line. "No, I'm not dead, Chief Inspector, but I agree that the situation requires some explaining, and that's what I would like to do. You see, I feel responsible in a way for what has happened. However, I have to consider my present wife and my family, for whom publicity could be most unpleasant."

"Is that the reason you've taken so long in getting in touch with me, sir?" Tansey asked. "Your fear of publicity?"

"Indeed not. We've been abroad for the last month. We've bought a cottage in Normandy and have been working hard on it, not bothering with English news — the papers aren't sold in the village — and it was an awful blow to come home to this tragedy."

"I see. Well, I'm prepared to meet you, sir, if it can be arranged, but I haven't the time to go to Scotland and I imagine you don't want to come to Police Headquarters here."

"Actually, my wife and I are in Oxford, staying at the Randolph, and I wondered if you'd be good enough to call on us there."

"This afternoon?"

"That would be fine, Chief Inspector. Three-thirty to four. Perhaps we can offer you tea, as it's an informal occasion."

"That's very kind of you. Thank you," said Tansey, noting that, in Vail's eyes, the meeting was to be off the record. He would have to be disabused of that idea.

★ ★ ★

Tansey didn't know what he had expected. Indeed when Lionel Vail met him in the hall of the Randolph Hotel he was doubting if he should have committed himself to this so-called unofficial mission. Vail was grey-haired and in his sixties, but there was no doubt he did closely resemble the photographs Tansey had seen of Oliver. However, his greeting was pleasant and affable, neither too friendly, nor too distant.

He led the way to a secluded corner of

284

the residents' lounge and said, "If I may, I'll tell you my story before my wife joins us and we have tea. The story is also to a great extent Oliver's." Vail was not as relaxed as he would have liked to seem; he had crossed his legs and one foot tapped steadily at the air. "I have to say at once that though I'm not proud of what I did, I can't bring myself to regret it — except for Oliver."

"Mr Vail, why are you telling me this?" Tansey interrupted. He wanted to make the position clear. "You must realize that I'm here as a police officer, and if you provide me with evidence relevant to the murder of your ex-wife I cannot treat it as a confidence."

"Chief Inspector, I thought I had made it plain. I haven't seen Lydia or Oliver or communicated with them for years. I know nothing about the murder except what I've learnt from the media but, because of the circumstances I'm hoping to explain to you, I feel I owe Oliver, and I need your advice."

"All right, Mr Vail. Go ahead." Tansey couldn't imagine why this man should need his advice. "I'll certainly listen."

"Well, it was like this . . . " Lionel Vail's quizzical smile showed that his choice of his opening words had been in deliberate mimicry of the average witness. "I was in my late forties, living with my wife Lydia and my son Oliver on the Isle of Wight, and practising my profession. We were a moderately happy family. As I said, I was a successful chartered accountant, putting in long hours at the office, but I enjoyed my work and was a contented man — until I met Rosemary and we fell desperately in love with each other."

"Rosemary was a widow with a small daughter. She had divorced her husband four years ago — he had been a brute — and soon after he had committed suicide, resulting in an unpleasant scandal. We knew our affair couldn't be kept a secret for ever, and in fact we were careless and Rosemary became pregnant." Vail sighed. "I asked Lydia for a divorce. Her answer was to say that if I didn't give up Rosemary she would resuscitate the scandal of Rosemary's husband and accuse me of unspeakable behaviour, all of which would ruin my reputation."

Vail was silent as he recalled his past, his face set in grim lines. Tansey was sympathetic. He waited without speaking. And with another sigh Vail continued.

"Eventually I told Lydia that I proposed to leave her. Rosemary and I had agreed that whatever she did we would have to face it. However, Lydia had second thoughts and sprung a surprise on me."

"Lydia was proud. She didn't love me, but she couldn't bear the thought of everyone knowing that she had been abandoned for another younger and more attractive woman. So, she offered me a bargain. I was to get another job, which wouldn't be too difficult, and Lydia was supposedly to follow me when our house had been sold. Actually, we were to part company. She was to settle wherever she wished. It turned out to be in Little Chipping. Our lawyers would arrange a quiet divorce and we would drop our Isle of Wight friends and connections and start new, separate lives. Chief Inspector, it was only when I read about Lydia's death that I realized she had decided to become a — a widow, apparently with a capital 'W'."

"Even if you had known, surely it wouldn't have made any difference to you?"

Tansey's interest in Vail's story was minimal. There was nothing unusual about it — a supposedly great romance and a vindictive wife, except that in the end Lydia Vail seemed to have behaved quite reasonably. If she had punished anyone it had been herself.

"To me personally, no, but to Oliver, yes. Lydia was always a possessive mother, and this is where I blame myself. I agreed never to see or communicate with Oliver again. I had to lie to him, suggest that I was seriously ill and make him promise to take care of Lydia whatever happened. Then, while he was away at boarding-school Lydia informed his headmaster that I had died but she didn't want Oliver to come home for the funeral. And by these means she became the Widow, saved her pride and bound Oliver yet more tightly to her."

As Vail finished speaking Rosemary Vail joined them. She was followed by a waiter with a laden tea-trolley. The second Mrs Vail was some fifteen years younger than her husband, a not unattractive middle-aged woman with a good, well-preserved figure.

When introductions had been completed and the three of them were seated, Mrs Vail poured tea and said, "Has Lionel explained our problem to you, Chief Inspector?"

"Your problem?" Tansey frowned. "No, not really, unless it's your wish to avoid all publicity connected with Oliver Vail, which is not unreasonable but no concern of mine."

"Indeed we would like that, for our own sakes," Rosemary Vail admitted honestly, "but also because of my daughter, who is soon to get married, and our two young sons."

"But Oliver must be given all possible help," Vail said. "Rosemary and I are agreed on that, and that's where we need your advice, Chief Inspector. If I were to be called as a defence witness and explained Oliver's relationship to Lydia and me, would it count as a mitigating circumstance? Is there any chance he might get a lighter sentence?"

"Mr Vail, I'm a police officer, not a lawyer. I don't know. It might. It would certainly win him sympathy in the media." Tansey paused. It was not his business, but — "I would suggest you wait until Oliver has been found." He didn't say that Oliver might already be dead. "Then, if my Chief Constable, who will have to be told your story, agrees, I'll try to arrange a meeting between you and Oliver. That's the best I can do."

The Vails were duly grateful and, driving back to Kidlington, Tansey decided that the afternoon had not been wasted. He felt that he now understood Oliver Vail much better than he had before.

18

HAVING been side-tracked from his journey to Little Chipping the previous afternoon by his appointment to meet with Lionel Vail, Tansey set off early next morning, accompanied by Abbot. It was a grey day with a hint of rain on the wind, and the temperature had dropped five degrees overnight. Nevertheless, they found Fred Denham stripped to the waist and chopping wood in his back garden.

The first point Tansey observed about him was the entwined snakes tattooed on both lower arms. Otherwise, Denham's resemblance to the man who had sold Mrs Vail's jewellery as described by Grove, the pawnbroker in Reading, was minimal. Granted, his hair was medium brown and his eyes light in colour, but he was not particularly tall and no one would have called his lop-sided face good-looking. He greeted the detectives without surprise, almost with a mixture of relief and apprehension, which was echoed by his words.

"I thought you'd be coming to see me," he said. "If you hadn't I was making up my mind to go to you. Not that it will help you much, but I suppose it might clear up a loose end, as it were."

"You're talking about your visit to Mrs Vail the evening she was killed, are you, Mr Denham?" Tansey was tentative.

"That's right. I didn't want to get involved, have to explain what I was doing there. It was nobody's business but my own, and if I'd not been fool enough to drop my tie nobody would need to have known about it. But I was that angry with the old bitch — "

Denham stopped abruptly. He hadn't put down his axe and now he split a log with unnecessary force. Tansey and Abbot exchanged glances; clearly Meg Denham's husband was not such a mild man as he had been portrayed. The ferocity of his retrospective anger was apparent.

"Anyways," Denham went on, "Meg's

been nagging at me about the tie, what was it doing there, and once the Reverend started asking questions, well — But it was Elaine's death that really made up my mind. I didn't care a damn about the Widow — good riddance — but Elaine was a fine girl. Last winter when Meg had the flu, she came in and worked for us and helped with the kids, till Meg was back on her feet again."

"You think the two murders are connected, Mr Denham?" Tansey wondered if they were to continue the interview — if it could be called that — in the garden. "Why?"

"I don't know, but whatever the papers seem to say I don't believe it was Oliver, and the second killing sort of proves it, doesn't it?"

If Denham's logic was faulty the sentiment was genuine, and Tansey reminded himself that the confession Oliver had made in his letter to Katie Sorel was not public property as yet. But they were being side-tracked again. He thought for a moment and then nodded at Abbot to intervene. Denham's attention appeared to be focused on the log he had just split.

Abbot said, "Mr Denham, that evening you visited Mrs Vail — what time did you get there?"

"Five-forty? I left home at the half-hour and it wouldn't have taken me long, just from the other end of the village. I walked fast."

"And you were there how long?"

"Say five minutes or so. Long enough for her to tell me what she thought of me. She said I was a scrounger, a ne'er-do-well, lazy, good-for-nothing, living on her taxes and making my wife go out to work. It was that last what really hurt. God knows I've done my best to get work."

Denham's voice broke, and he swallowed hard. "That was why I was there, wasn't I, begging the Widow for a job? Meg had told me the house could do with a paint job. But the Widow said if her house did need painting she wouldn't employ someone on the dole — as if I'd damn well chosen to be on the bloody dole. Then she slammed the door in my face." Denham drew a deep breath that came out as a burp. "I can guess what you're thinking, but I didn't kill her, though I could have done."

Tansey gave Denham a chance to vent his anger on another log before he said, "What were you wearing, Mr Denham?"

"What was I — ? Oh, you mean the tie. Yes, I'd dressed up for the occasion. Slacks and a jacket, clean shirt and tie. I didn't intend to give her the chance to call me a slob, though why I went to that trouble — " Denham couldn't hide his bitterness. "Anyways, I was furious. She had no right to treat me like dirt. Without thinking I pulled off my tie — I'm not that used to wearing the wretched things — and put it in my pocket. I suppose it must have fallen out. How it got on the rhododendron where Meg found it I've no idea. I never put it there."

"Mrs Vail's next caller saw it on the ground and picked it up," Tansey explained.

"Ah!" Denham wasn't really interested.

"Did anyone see you coming or going that evening?"

Denham frowned, apparently not understanding the drift of the question. "No, I don't think so. I saw Tom Sorel in the distance as I was leaving. You could ask him, but I'm fairly sure he didn't see me, and I wasn't in the mood to talk to anyone at that point so I didn't even wave."

"You saw no one else?"

"Not until I got down into the village. There were a few people about there, but I went straight home."

"Right. Thank you, Mr Denham. We'll let you get on with your work then."

Relieved, Fred Denham saw them to the back gate and watched them depart. Tansey was shaking his head.

"Poor devil," he said. "It must be hell to be on the dole for years."

"Sir, my parents were saying their house needed painting. Would it be out of order if I asked them to employ Denham?"

"Of course not. That would be great. Denham's not a suspect, Sergeant, though we'll check with Tom Sorel. Let's get on to Colombury and see if he's about."

★ ★ ★

The cottage where old Mrs Sorel lived with her son Tom, when he was at home, was identical to Katie's but the front room was comfortably furnished. Tansey sat in an armchair, and Sorel, looking very much at ease, sprawled on a divan where Tansey suspected he slept. They were alone. Abbot had gone off to visit his parents and persuade them to give Fred Denham a painting job. Old Mrs Sorel was in the kitchen.

"I thought you'd be along to interrogate me sooner or later, Chief Inspector," Sorel said.

"Really? Why?"

As Sorel rearranged a cushion behind his back the sleeve of his sweater rode up and Tansey saw part of a tattoo on his arm. But Sorel fitted the pawnbroker's description of the man who had sold him Mrs Vail's jewellery little better than Denham did. He was tall and definitely handsome — Tansey recalled that a girl in the Windrush Arms had said his nickname was 'The Smasher' — but his hair was fair, his face thin, his manner arrogant.

"I assumed you'd be after anyone who had ever been one of Elaine Pulman's lovers. Mind you, it's nothing to be proud of. She was quite a girl and she got around."

"When was this, Mr Sorel?" From the way Elaine had spoken of Tom Sorel, Tansey wondered if there was any truth in his assertion or if it was merely the boasting of a vain man.

"Ages ago, when she first came to Little Chipping. Before I had a wife."

"I gather you don't have a wife now."

"No, unfortunately. It was my fault. I neglected her, but I didn't have much choice. If you're at sea you can't come home every night to keep the little woman warm. But things change. She's had her fling with Oliver Vail, and maybe she'll give me a second chance."

This sounded honest enough, but Tansey distrusted it; it was not the picture painted by Katie and Elaine, or by the Reverend Basil Moore. Nevertheless, Sorel was entitled to his hopes.

Tansey changed the subject. "In fact, Mr Sorel, you've misunderstood why I've come to see you," he said mildly. "My reason was to ask for your help."

"Helping the police with their inquiries?" There was a sour note in Sorel's voice.

Tansey ignored it. "Throw your mind back to the Wednesday evening that Mrs Vail was killed, Mr Sorel, please. Did you see anyone in the vicinity of the house when you were around there?"

Sorel stared at him, his eyes cold. "No, I did not, Chief Inspector, because I was nowhere near the Vails' house that evening. I'd only got back to Colombury the day before after months away. I visited my ex-wife and my daughter that afternoon. Afterwards, I went home and stayed there. You can ask my ma. I was a bit upset, so I didn't go to the pub as I might have done. Katie hadn't been exactly welcoming, and my poor little Joy's health was no better."

It was a long explanation, Tansey thought, too long perhaps. "Someone believes he saw you near the Vails' place," he said, "around five forty-five."

"Then he was wrong. He was mistaken or he's a liar." Sorel's temper flared. "I was nowhere near there that evening."

It was a flat denial, and there was no point in arguing about it; after all, Fred Denham could have been mistaken or he could even have lied. "In which case I won't bother you any more," Tansey said, getting to his feet. "I was hoping you might be able to confirm what this witness had told me, but it's not important. Many thanks for bearing with me, Mr Sorel."

"That's OK, Chief Inspector. You're only doing your duty."

Sorel had also risen from his divan, and he grinned as if to deny any impression he might have conveyed that the remark was meant to be patronizing, but it was a thoughtful Chief Inspector who walked down the lane to find Abbot. Not that he was allowed much time to ruminate on Tom Sorel's character. Abbot greeted him with the news that Oliver Vail had walked into the police station in Ryde, Isle of Wight, and given himself up. Inspector Whitelaw was arranging for him to be taken over to Portsmouth on the ferry under police escort; there he would be met by a car from Headquarters at Kidlington.

"He should arrive in the early evening, sir," Abbot said.

★ ★ ★

In the event Oliver Vail was brought into Tansey's office shortly after six o'clock. His appearance was something of a shock. His fair hair had been dyed a dark brown, he wore spectacles and he walked with a stick. But his clothes, though crumpled, were typical of the former respected bank official; he wore a dark grey suit, white shirt and a plain blue tie.

Before Tansey could do more than motion him to the chair in front of his desk Oliver said, "I'm sorry for all the trouble I've caused you, but after — after what happened I desperately needed a few days to myself, somewhere where I had been happy, somewhere I could remember for the next twenty-five years or however long you're going to lock me up."

"Well, you're here now, Mr Vail. I'm told you've been given the official warning that whatever you say may be used against you, and that you've refused a lawyer, at least for the moment. Is that correct?"

"Yes, that's right.

"Then I shall turn on this tape-recorder, and Detective-Sergeant Abbot over there will take notes. And I hope that, after I've made a preliminary announcement for the benefit of the recording, you'll give us an account of what happened on the evening your mother was killed, and what you did afterwards."

"I'll do my best."

"Fine!" Tansey nodded encouragement, and after a slight pause for the formalities, Oliver Vail began.

"I collected the Jaguar from the Windrush Garage in Colombury as it was shutting, around six o'clock. I drove around for a bit. I was worried. Katie, my girl, had said she was tired of waiting, either we got married or she wouldn't see me any more, but it wasn't easy. I couldn't leave Mother, and she didn't approve of Katie because she had been divorced." Oliver stopped, frowning at his thoughts. "But I must stick to facts."

According to Oliver he had driven home, left the car outside because he thought his mother would want to inspect it, and gone into the house. He had called out that he was home, and when there was no reply he had looked into the sitting-room.

"It was awful," he said, "dreadful — like something out of a horror movie. I stood and stared. She'd always said that one day we'd have a burglar which is why she kept the rifle, but why didn't he just tie her up and take what he wanted? No. I suppose she must have been upstairs and heard someone and come down with the gun and threatened him, and instead of bolting as she expected he attacked her. She was in a dreadful state — but you must have seen her. Her head was battered — blood and brains all over the place — and, what's more, the room was smeared with her blood. I knew she was dead, that no one could be alive in that state, that nothing could be done. Then, suddenly, I saw her twitch. It was — was a nightmare."

"Twitch?" said the Chief Inspector, thinking of Dr Ghent's reaction that Thursday morning when a trick of light had made the body seem to move.

"Yes, twitch. And then she sort of twitched again, and I knew what I must do. I promised my father when he knew he was going to die that I would always look after her, and I couldn't leave her in this needless agony. Maybe it was madness, but I picked up the rifle and shot her to make sure she was out of her misery. I killed my mother, Chief Inspector."

"All right, Mr Vail. All right," Tansey said soothingly. Oliver was shaking and he didn't want him to collapse. "Would you like something? A cup of tea?"

"No, thanks." After a minute Oliver continued. "I went to the cloakroom — "

"The downstairs cloakroom?" asked Tansey quickly.

"Yes. I washed my hands — several times, though I'd tried not to get any of her blood on me. Then I fled. The Jag was outside and I took it. My one purpose was to get away from that — that horror."

"I spent the night in the car in a lay-by near Wychwood. In the morning I thought of giving myself up, but I couldn't face all the fuss and the questions. I knew it wasn't possible, but I wanted to forget what had happened. Anyway, the idea came to me to go down to the Isle of Wight, just for a week. I drove to Reading. I took three hundred pounds out of my Colombury bank account. I sold the Jaguar. I bought a cheap rucksack and some clothes. I had nothing except what I was wearing — this suit, the one I had worn to the office the previous morning.

"I went down to the Island that afternoon. It was as wonderful as I remembered, and I was determined to have my week. But I knew the police would be looking for me, which is why I bought these spectacles and a walking-stick and some hair dye — easily obtainable at any chemists. I shan't need them any more now." He took off the spectacles and laid them on Tansey's desk; the walking stick was lying by his chair. "I spent one night in a big hotel, paid in advance, and left very early the next morning in my new disguise, before the day-shift receptionist who had checked me in came on duty. Then I booked into a smaller place, and spent my week exploring my old haunts.

"And that is that, Chief Inspector. I suppose my week cost the taxpayer a lot of money, but at least they'll recoup some of it by my pleading guilty, won't they?"

"That will have to be seen, Mr Vail. We've a long way to go. We haven't even charged you yet."

"No. Dear God! Nor you have. Why ever not?" Oliver Vail produced a pallid smile. "I'm sorry. I feel so tired."

Tansey hesitated. He was a compassionate man, and Oliver Vail certainly looked exhausted, but a Chief Inspector had to consider his duty. Tansey weighed the advantages of letting Oliver try to get a good night's sleep, so that he was fresh for further questioning in the morning, against pressing him hard now.

"All right," he said at length. "We'll call it a day, Mr Vail. You know we can detain you without charge for forty-eight hours or longer, in certain circumstances. In any case, this will give me a chance to review all you've told me."

But when Abbot had taken Oliver away Tansey didn't replay the tape.

He thought about Oliver Vail as a boy, the only child of a proud, possessive, vindictive mother, and a clever man who had abandoned him, and he wondered what effect Oliver's upbringing had had on his character. He was said to be a devoted son and a kind, considerate individual; Tansey remembered how he had paid Bert Bilson's rent that was owed to the Widow, arranged for Katie Sorel to take Joy to London specialists, even thought to buy the little girl a xylophone when he was on the run, and sent Katie the money from the sale of the Jaguar. And everyone had spoken well of him; there was no suggestion that he was other than what he seemed to be, a good, honest, possibly over-conscientious young man.

So, was he capable of inventing the story he had just recounted? Anyway, why invent it? Why admit to shooting his mother, but not to assaulting her? Why not deny both?

Hopeful that the next day would provide answers to some of the questions that disturbed him, Chief Inspector Tansey decided to go home.

19

"LET'S go through it once more," Tansey said.

Oliver Vail gritted his teeth; he had been 'going through it' and answering questions for the whole morning. Either they believed him or they didn't. He was beyond caring. Apart from his beloved Katie he had no regrets, but he wished the entire sorry business was over. A prison cell wouldn't be as pleasant as his time on the Isle of Wight, but it would be peaceful in comparison with his present situation.

"I don't understand about your clothes, Mr Vail," Tansey said.

Oliver sighed. "What is there to understand? I had been at work, at the bank. I was wearing a business suit. I went home. I found that dreadful — scene. I fled. In Reading I bought some inexpensive things, which I've worn during the last week. They're in my rucksack, which I'm sure you've searched."

"I don't understand why there isn't at least some blood on your suit if that's the one you were wearing when you killed your mother."

Oliver didn't wince. He was getting hardened. "I told you. I picked up the rifle with great care."

"It was lying beside her? On which side?"

"On her left side, as I said before. I didn't go upstairs to fetch it. I didn't attack her."

"You just shot her — with the second bullet?"

"The second bullet? What do you mean?" His surprise seemed genuine.

"There was a bullet in the wall. Did you try the rifle to make sure it worked, say?"

"No!"

"All right, Mr Vail. After the shooting you went upstairs to wash?"

"You've asked me that before. I did not go upstairs to wash or to change my clothes or to pack a going-away bag or for any other reason. How many more times, Chief Inspector?"

"You didn't take your mother's jewellery?"

Oliver shook his head, brushing aside the suggestion as absurd. "I went straight from the sitting-room to the downstairs cloakroom. I washed and left the house."

"You washed. Had you cut yourself, Mr Vail?"

This was a new question, and Oliver showed his surprise. "How did you know? Actually I hadn't cut myself, but I was shaking and I caught my finger under the tap, which was sharp — and it bled like anything. But why is that important?"

Tansey didn't reply, but he realized that Oliver had just explained the fact that Dr Ghent, the pathologist, had found a different type of blood in the cloakroom, and the point helped to confirm Oliver's account of events.

The questions continued. Their order was varied, but the answers remained consistent and, by lunch time, when Oliver was taken back to his cell, Tansey was convinced he had been speaking the truth.

Chief Inspector Tansey had a busy afternoon. First, accompanied by Inspector Whitelaw and Sergeant Abbot, he took Oliver Vail to Little Chipping and his former home. Oliver had objected; he never wanted to go near the place again. But Tansey had been adamant.

Although the media and the locals had by now lost interest in this scene of a horrible crime, the house and garden were still cordoned off, and there was a round-the-clock police guard on the property. Oliver regarded these precautions dubiously, and when they got out of the car he balked.

"Chief Inspector, I can't face going in."

"You must, Mr Vail." Tansey was firm. "There's nothing unpleasant to see."

Whitelaw unlocked the back door and said, "You say you can't remember if this door was locked when you returned home on the evening your mother was killed, Mr Vail?"

"No, I can't remember but, as I

311

said before, there would be nothing odd whether it was or not. The latch was usually down, but if Mother heard me arrive she would sometimes put it up for me."

"All right, Mr Vail. Come along in," Tansey said.

He led the way along the passage and up the stairs, which were covered so that no bloodstains were to be seen, nor the bare patches where areas of carpet had been cut away, to the door of Oliver's bedroom, where he let Oliver go ahead of him. Oliver went in hesitantly, but the room had been tidied after the police search and looked much as it always had done.

Oliver frowned. "I don't understand. Why have you brought me here?"

"We'd like you to inspect your clothes and tell us if anything is missing."

"As you wish." Oliver began in a desultory fashion, but soon was probing in earnest. He turned indignantly to the watching detectives. "My new blouson has gone. Mother didn't like it. She was conventional about clothes. But I did. And there's a new pair of slacks missing, too. Have you taken them?"

"No," Tansey said. "Are you sure they're gone? Perhaps they've fallen to the floor of the wardrobe."

Obediently Oliver scrabbled among the shoes on the base of the cupboard and produced a pair of jeans and a shirt. He looked at them in disgust. Then he suddenly threw them at Tansey's feet.

"These aren't mine. I never wear jeans. I find them uncomfortable. And if this is some kind of trick, as I suppose it is, I think it's insufferable."

Tansey picked up the jeans. They were not the original bloodstained ones found in the rabbit hole by the lawyer's dachshund — those were still with Forensic — but they were as much like them in colour and size as WPC Norton had been able to find that morning. Tansey held them out to Oliver.

"Mr Vail, it is a trick, and for that I apologize, but I assure you it's not aimed at you. On the contrary. Would you please try these jeans on?"

"Very well!" Oliver did his best, but after a minute it was clear that the jeans were too small for him around the waist, and at least two inches too long. "Now what?" he demanded.

"That's all, thank you." Tansey was brisk, and didn't show his pleasure. "If you'd like to change and put on some clean clothes we'll leave you with Sergeant Abbot."

★ ★ ★

While they waited for Oliver Vail and Abbot the Chief Inspector put through a series of phone calls from his car. Since Oliver hadn't killed his mother, and by now there was proof of his innocence, who had? And who had killed Elaine? There were several possibilities, but to the Chief Inspector one man in particular had suddenly become the most likely. However, before any accusations were made — even before an interrogation — he had some checking to do.

He phoned Katie Sorel and asked her how she had spent the evening that Mrs Vail had been killed. Surprised, she said that shortly after Oliver had gone to collect the Jaguar, she had left the cottage to have supper with her friend

314

Monica Carter and had spent the evening with the Carters. Tansey then told her, since it would be on the late news and in the following day's papers, that Oliver was safe and well, though in custody in Oxford.

He spoke to Sidney Corbet who, with a little prompting, recalled a good deal more of what Elaine had said about her time in the woods behind the Vails' house with Paul Smith. He too produced the hoped-for answers.

He gave WPC Norton instructions to check on certain police records in the Met's central computer and, if a prison record was found, to obtain all the particulars, and to make sure by confirming with the police force where the convictions had taken place, personal details, such as physical description, blood group and so on. For answers to these queries he would have to wait, and he cursed himself for not having done this before, when the evidence of prison pallor was before his eyes.

He spoke to the Chief Constable's secretary and asked for half an hour of his time late that afternoon. Finally, when

Inspector Whitelaw had got out of the car to stretch his legs and make sure that Sergeant Donaldson's men were guarding the property efficiently, he phoned Lionel Vail with the news of his son, Oliver. This was an off-the-record call, but Tansey put it down not as an act of charity but as a way of maintaining a good relationship between the police and the public. He assured Lionel Vail that there was no need for him yet to take any action. He knew the Chief Constable would approve.

Whitelaw returned soon after Tansey had finished his calls, followed by Oliver, looking relaxed in jacket and slacks, and Abbot who carried a weekend bag containing more of Oliver's clothes and toiletries and a plastic carrier bag that held the business suit Oliver had been wearing. And as they set off back to Headquarters Tansey thought that the next thirty-six hours were going to be all-important to a variety of people.

★ ★ ★

Tansey spent the rest of the afternoon re-reading the files, making yet more

316

telephone calls, considering the fresh information which WPC Norton was producing and preparing for his report to the Chief Constable. By five o'clock when he was to go to Philip Midvale's office, he believed that he had a case against the killer of the Widow and Elaine Pulman — a case that could be made acceptable to the Crown Prosecution Service. He hoped that Midvale would agree.

"You've seen all the reports, including my own, sir," Tansey said. "I've tried to produce a coherent story, taking into account some new information I've received. As I understand it now, sir, this is what happened." With a brief glance at his notes, the Chief Inspector began his exposition. "There is some surmise, but mostly it's factual and can be corroborated."

"Right. Go ahead, Chief Inspector." Midvale shifted in his chair; his arthritis was troubling him this evening.

"Vic Rowe, the gardener, left the Vails' house at four-forty, after a brief altercation over the time he had worked. This is relevant only because it shows that Mrs Vail was not in the best of tempers.

317

Then Fred Denham, the painter, came asking for work about five forty-five, and was verbally abused. He was there about five minutes and, leaving, saw Tom Sorel in the distance, but Sorel didn't see him.

"The next arrival at the house, at approximately six o'clock, was Mrs Vail's killer. And here I have to guess, sir. I believe he rang the back doorbell, but it doesn't work well, and Mrs Vail who had almost certainly gone upstairs didn't hear it. He saw an open window and, thinking no one was at home — he may have looked in the garage and seen that the car wasn't there — seized his chance and entered the house. Upstairs, Mrs Vail heard someone moving about. Perhaps he knocked something over. She knew it wasn't Oliver because Oliver always called out that he was back. She took the rifle that she kept in expectation of a thief breaking in and went downstairs to confront him."

As Tansey paused to marshal his thoughts the Chief Constable said, "That's a reasonable scenario so far, but why does this thief kill Mrs Vail? Surely he could have knocked her down and run?"

"She would have recognized him."

"Even so?"

"She was not in a good temper, and even at her best she was not a forgiving character. I imagine she lashed him with her tongue as she had done earlier to Fred Denham and threatened him with prison. What she didn't know was that he had just come out of gaol and had no intention of returning there. At any rate they struggled for the rifle, and a shot went into the wall. Then he must have lost his temper and brutally killed her.

"Which means the murder was unpremeditated."

"I think that's a moot point, sir. Temper or not, it could be argued that if he were to avoid another, longer sentence, he had no alternative but to do away with her. Further, there's no doubt that Elaine Pulman's murder was premeditated and planned. I'll be coming to that later, sir."

The Chief Constable nodded and looked meaningfully at his watch. He was going out to dinner later and he wanted to get home and have a good soak in a hot bath to ease his aches and pains. The gesture was not lost on Tansey. He hurried on.

"The murderer went upstairs — it was him Thane, the poulterer, heard washing around six twenty-five — changed into some clothes of Oliver's, stole loose cash and jewellery and left, with his bloodstained things that he later buried. By chance, Elaine Pulman saw him leave but, not knowing he was back in Colombury, decided she must be mistaken and it was Oliver. At a distance the two men are not unalike.

"In fact, Oliver didn't arrive home until about ten to seven. Janice Moore saw him drive off about ten past. He did not kill his mother, sir. She was dead by the time he shot her. It was a trick of the light reflected in a mirror that made him believe she moved. Dr Ghent had the same experience the next morning. I believe Oliver when he suggests that it was a kind of mercy killing, which in fact we now know wasn't a killing at all. But when Oliver fled and the media decided he was guilty, the real killer must have been delighted.

"How he learnt that Elaine had seen him at the Vails' house, but thought he was Oliver, I don't know. She told the Corbets about it. She may have told Katie Sorel. Anyway, he did learn of it, and he was afraid she might change her mind and decide she hadn't made a mistake about the identity of the man she saw. He knew she was a risk. He was in The Windrush Arms the night Elaine and Katie and Monica Carter went in for a drink after the cinema, and he could have heard she was walking back to Little Chipping alone. I believe he collected one of his mother's scarves, followed Elaine and killed her."

"What about hard evidence, Chief Inspector?"

"For Elaine's murder, none at the moment, sir. For Mrs Vail's, a great deal. There's another witness, whom he didn't know about, who saw him near the scene of the crime at the right time, but he denies being there, and when he said his mother could give him an alibi for that evening he was lying, because from six o'clock she was babysitting for Katie Sorel's little girl while Katie was at the Carters'. Most important, we shall be able to prove that the bloodstained clothes which the murderer wore were his and that the so far unidentified blood and tissue found in the Vails' house were also his. And I'm sure Grove, the pawnbroker, will identify him, though he did a certain amount to disguise himself."

"Right. That should be enough to be going on with. But have you any idea why he was near the Vails' house in the first place?"

"I believe he went to challenge Oliver, to threaten him perhaps, if he didn't stop seeing Katie Sorel. He wanted Katie back."

"I see. Well, what do you want, Chief Inspector?"

"Sir, to take Tom Sorel in for questioning tomorrow morning. To search Granny Sorel's cottage; we may need a warrant for that. And we'll certainly need one to arrest Sorel for the murders of Lydia Vail and Elaine Pulman. I know the case concerning Elaine is thin at the moment, but I'm hoping he may break under questioning."

Philip Midvale nodded slowly. "Right,"

he said again. "But what about Oliver?"

"We must certainly keep him till we've picked up Sorel, for if Sorel sees him on the loose, he'll guess that the game is up. For the future, I've an idea how to deal with Oliver — an idea which, if you agree, will be in everyone's best interests."

"Tell me," said the Chief Constable, thinking regretfully of the hot bath he had promised himself.

20

THERE was to be much recrimination about exactly what happened the next day. Tansey was to blame himself, but it was no more his fault than Whitelaw's or WPC Norton's or even the Chief Constable's. They all contributed, as did Sergeant Donaldson, plus some accidents that could not have been foreseen.

Tansey arrived at Headquarters at eight-thirty. To his surprise Philip Midvale was already there. The previous evening he had agreed with Tansey about the procedure to be followed as far as Oliver Vail was concerned, and the arrangements for taking Tom Sorel into custody. But this morning it seemed he had had second thoughts. At any rate, he wanted to run through the routine again.

Tansey bore the delay stoically. The Chief Constable looked as if he hadn't slept much and this morning was finding it difficult to hide the fact that he was in considerable pain. He will be retiring soon, Tansey thought, and we'll be lucky if his replacement is half as good at his job and half as understanding.

But time was passing, and he was thankful when Midvale had been satisfied, and he could return to his office and send for Oliver Vail. He had instructed Inspector Whitelaw to go on ahead to Colombury with WPC Norton, and to enlist the support of Sergeant Donaldson and any men he had available, if he thought it necessary. Tansey had added, "But don't phone Donaldson in advance and warn him you're coming and that we're about to make a search and take someone into custody; if you do the news'll be half over the town by the time you get there." He wished he could have sent Sergeant Abbot with them, but Abbot's wife had phoned in to say her husband was in bed with the prevalent summer flu.

"Good morning, Mr Vail," Tansey said as Oliver was brought in. "Please sit down."

"Good morning, Chief Inspector; at least it would be nice if it were good." Oliver sounded resigned. "More questions?"

"No, Mr Vail, I don't think so. Rather it's information I have to give you — information which will be a surprise." Tansey paused, but there was no way of telling Oliver except bluntly. "First, you did not kill your mother, and this morning we are going to take into custody the man we believe did."

Oliver stared at him, his mouth half open, as Tansey explained the situation, and especially the trick of the light which had caused Oliver to believe that Lydia Vail had moved. He shook his head in bewilderment.

"Oh God, I'm glad," he said at last. "I hated shooting her, but I thought — she seemed in such dreadful pain and I had promised my father . . . But does this mean I don't have to stand trial and go to prison?"

"That's right. It wouldn't be worth bringing you to trial for what you did do, Mr Vail. No jury would convict you, with the real culprit already found guilty. So what the Chief Constable has in mind is that a formal statement of your innocence

326

should be made to the media and your — er — running away be explained as a result of shock at finding your mother in such a condition. This subsequently resulted in some loss of memory. Would you accept that?"

"Yes. Yes. It's wonderful!" Oliver was having difficulty taking in what had happened. "I'll be able to marry Katie now, and look after little Joy." He gave Tansey a wry smile. "And live happily ever after."

"Mr Vail, there'll be problems. You'll probably have to appear in court as a witness, and — "

"I can guess, Chief Inspector. But what you've told me is such a relief. I'll cope with the problems. When can I go?"

"This afternoon or early evening, when the alleged killer is safely in custody."

"But who? Who?"

"Mr Vail, I can't tell you that at present. But I have more news for you. It concerns your father."

Perhaps Oliver Vail had had enough for one morning, for he took what Tansey had to tell him about Lionel calmly, admitting that he would need time to get used to the idea. But it was obvious that he was deeply moved, and Tansey left him with a collection of newspapers, and a promise that later on in the day he would be allowed to speak to Katie Sorel and his father.

★ ★ ★

When Inspector Whitelaw arrived in Colombury with WPC Norton, he found that a private car — a Ford Escort XR3, which he recognized as Sergeant Donaldson's personal vehicle — was parked facing the wrong way and occupying the one reserved space outside the police station. Irritated, Whitelaw was forced to park at the rear of the building. Perhaps this made him more brusque than was necessary. He told Donaldson that they were taking Tom Sorel in for questioning about the Vail affair, and that they were going to search old Mrs Sorel's cottage. They needed the help of two officers.

Donaldson was not cooperative. He said he didn't have the men, and it was true that the local force was badly stretched, but somehow he managed to imply that an Inspector and a WPC should have been able to cope with the job. Whitelaw insisted, and reluctantly Donaldson agreed to come himself. The three of them walked down Green Lane to the cottage where Granny Sorel lived.

She opened the door to them, and when they had explained their business, said, "Tom's not here and I don't know where he is."

"We'd like to come in and look around," Whitelaw said.

"Well, I'm not sure — "

"We have a search warrant," Donaldson interrupted.

Silently Whitelaw cursed the sergeant for his lack of tact. The old lady was already perturbed, and he didn't want a charge of intimidation brought against them. There was a young man leaning against the wall of the next cottage taking in everything that was going on, who would probably be happy to be a witness to police brutality.

"It's all right, Mrs Sorel," Whitelaw said soothingly.

But WPC Norton had stepped forward. "Perhaps you'd show me upstairs, Mrs

Sorel," she said. "How big is your cottage? I used to live in one rather like it when I was a child."

Without realizing what was happening Granny Sorel found herself leading WPC Norton up the steep narrow stairs to her bedroom. Whitelaw sent Donaldson to the back premises, and himself went into the front room. The search began. WPC Norton was not lucky, though she did discover that Granny Sorel had a collection of silk scarves. But Whitelaw had just located a loose floorboard underneath the divan when he heard Donaldson calling to him.

Donaldson was in an outhouse, a lean-to attached to the back of the cottage. He met Whitelaw at the door. He was exuding triumph.

"Look what I've found, sir," he said. "See that old scarecrow. Funny place for a scarecrow, isn't it?"

In fact, the object to which he pointed had never been intended as a scarecrow. Quite obviously it was one of those adjustable wire needlewoman's dummies that Katie Sorel had probably used years ago to fashion whatever garment she was making. Now, wearing some cast-off clothing and swathed in a dirty blanket, it did perhaps resemble a scarecrow but, contrary to what Donaldson had claimed, it wasn't in the least out of place amid the bits and pieces of junk that filled the outhouse.

"Try undressing it, sir," suggested Donaldson.

Whitelaw obliged and a minute later emitted a low whistle, for beneath the blanket and some tattered clothing was revealed a dark blue blouson, surely the property of Oliver Vail. Whitelaw had to give Donaldson full marks for thoroughness; he could easily have ignored the so-called scarecrow. But it was Whitelaw himself who looked in the pockets of the blouson and found several pieces of jet jewellery that Tom Sorel had been unable to sell in Reading.

Their triumph was to be short-lived. Almost immediately from further down the lane towards the High Street there came a series of violent screams, expressive of both fear and anger. They ran, almost colliding with WPC Norton at the foot of the stairs. Granny Sorel was putting on the kettle in the kitchen, a look of quiet satisfaction on her face.

★ ★ ★

WPC Norton, who had a university degree and high hopes of a successful career in the police, had been tricked by an uneducated old woman three times her age.

"Would you mind if I went down and made us all a cup of tea, dear?" Granny Sorel had asked.

At that point WPC Norton was perched precariously on a rickety chair in an attempt to inspect the top of the wardrobe. Distracted, she muttered assent, and Mrs Sorel went heavily downstairs. There was no one about. Quietly she opened the front door and spoke rapidly to the young man who was still propping up the wall next door. He disappeared down the lane and banged on Katie Sorel's door.

"Is Tom here?"

"Yes. He's in the kitchen. Why?"

The young man, whose name was Peter Mace, barged past Katie into the kitchen, startling Tom and Joy. "Your ma sent me to warn you, Tom," he said. "The fuzz have turned up in force. There's three of them searching the cottage, and they're after you. They've got a warrant for your arrest. You'd better get out while you can."

This was not strictly true. The police only had a warrant to search the cottage. At this stage, they merely intended to take Tom in for questioning. But old Mrs Sorel had misunderstood, and Tom panicked. He hadn't been able to bring himself to dispose of Oliver's expensive blouson which he coveted, and he knew the police would find it if the search was thorough — and the remains of the Widow's jewellery which was still in its pocket. Useless to regret his decision to keep them now.

"Shall I see if there's a police car at the end of the lane?" Peter Mace asked. He was rather enjoying the situation.

"No. Don't bother." Tom's mind worked fast. There were often cars left unattended in the High Street while their owners were inside a shop. If he could nick one and get away before the fuzz realized he had gone, he could lay up with a tart he knew until he could get abroad. He wasn't going inside again, whatever happened; this time it would be a long stretch. It would be a third offence and serious, and there would be no guarantee of a lenient judge like the one who had let him off with two years last time. "Just keep Katie quiet, Peter."

Before Katie realized what Tom intended he had seized Joy and hurried out of the cottage. The little girl, he hoped, would help to divert suspicion, and later might be useful as a hostage, or if necessary he could always get rid of her; he would have no compunction.

But he had reckoned without Katie. Mace did his best to block her way, but in the circumstances he was no match for her. She bit his restraining hand and punched him in the stomach with all the force that her small frame could muster. Then she was out of the cottage running after her ex-husband and screaming furiously.

It was these screams of Katie's that caused Inspector Whitelaw, Sergeant

Donaldson and WPC Norton to come tearing out of Granny Smith's cottage and down the lane to the High Street. But none of them were in time to prevent Joy's abduction.

★ ★ ★

In spite of Katie's screams behind him Tom Sorel's luck held. Outside the police station was a Ford Escort, keys in the ignition, the door unlocked. Sergeant Donaldson's carelessness in leaving it to be stolen so easily was to earn him a reproof.

Tom Sorel pulled open the driver's door and thrust Joy across the seat before sliding behind the wheel. He started the engine and noted with pleasure that there was plenty of petrol in the tank, and for the moment there was almost no traffic on the street. He edged out of the parking space and put his foot down on the accelerator.

He didn't see Chief Inspector Dick Tansey. In the absence of Abbot, Tansey had driven himself to Colombury, had parked his car at the rear of the police station and had just returned to the front of the building when he saw Tom Sorel burst out of the lane carrying his small daughter. If Tansey had any doubts about the validity of Tom's actions they were dispelled by the sounds of screams and running footsteps and the brutal manner in which Tom Sorel threw Joy into the car.

Tansey's reaction was automatic. With a single thought in his mind — that Tom Sorel had to be stopped — he ran out across the road as Sorel accelerated. Somehow with one hand he managed to seize the car driver's door handle, and as the door swung open he grasped its frame with his other hand. He felt as if his arms were being pulled from their sockets.

By now Sorel, who had expected Tansey to fall off had realized that he must act and was trying to shut the door against Tansey's body and push him off at the same time. But the car was swinging dangerously from side to side of the street, the open door swinging with it. Tansey hung on for grim death and by some miracle both flying feet found the inside of the car, which promptly knocked a boy off his bicycle, scraped along the side panel of a van and spread-eagled the boxes of second-hand books outside a bookshop. There were shouts and screams, the hooting of car horns, a cacophony of sounds.

Tansey was now in a stronger position. He grabbed the steering-wheel and aimed a blow at Sorel with his other fist. By chance rather than intent he caught Sorel full in the face. Sorel, momentarily blinded, lost control of the car completely. It mounted the pavement and embedded itself in the front window of an off-licence. The whole incident had lasted less than a minute.

An angry and frustrated Inspector Whitelaw reached the scene moments later and knew he must take control. Tom Sorel was lifting a dazed head from the dashboard; he had a broken nose and blood was streaming down his face. Joy was sitting on the car floor, screaming loudly but apparently unharmed.

What shocked Inspector Whitelaw was the sight of Chief Inspector Richard Tansey. Dick Tansey, thrown from the car, lay in the gutter. He was a crumpled heap, his skin grey, his eyes not quite shut. He looked dead, but he was still breathing. Whitelaw, his voice tight, issued orders.

★ ★ ★

It was two days before Chief Inspector Tansey regained consciousness and several weeks before he was out of hospital and able to pay a visit to his headquarters. Meanwhile, thanks to the media and a tourist who had videoed most of the incident in Colombury, he had become something of a national hero and had been recommended for the Queen's Police Medal for Gallantry.

This he considered undeserved. "If only I hadn't been so blind, sir," he said to Chief Constable Philip Midvale, "I would have checked on Tom Sorel long before I did. But it was fixed in my mind that he had been at sea and had only just come home, and it didn't occur to me that he might have almost immediately gone to the Vails' place in search of Oliver."

"My dear Tansey, you can't expect

to be omniscient. Personally, I think you did splendidly. Oliver Vail's happy staying with his newly-found father. He and Katie are being married soon. Joy is safe and quite recovered from her experience. And, most importantly from the police point of view, Tom Sorel will be getting the long term in prison that he deserves. What more do you want?"

Midvale did not expect an answer to his question and Tansey didn't attempt to give him one, but he thought regretfully of Elaine Pulman and the people in Colombury and Little Chipping, especially the Corbets, who would miss her. He wished he had not wasted so much time looking in the wrong direction.

TO FIGHT THE WILD
Rod Ansell and Rachel Percy

Lost in uncharted Australian bush, Rod Ansell survived by hunting and trapping wild animals, improvising shelter and using all the bushman's skills he knew.

COROMANDEL
Pat Barr

India in the 1830s is a hot, uncomfortable place, where the East India Company still rules. Amelia and her new husband find themselves caught up in the animosities which seethe between the old order and the new.

THE SMALL PARTY
Lillian Beckwith

A frightening journey to safety begins for Ruth and her small party as their island is caught up in the dangers of armed insurrection.

THE WILDERNESS WALK
Sheila Bishop

Stifling unpleasant memories of a misbegotten romance in Cleave with Lord Francis Aubrey, Lavinia goes on holiday there with her sister. The two women are thrust into a romantic intrigue involving none other than Lord Francis.

THE RELUCTANT GUEST
Rosalind Brett

Ann Calvert went to spend a month on a South African farm with Theo Borland and his sister. They both proved to be different from her first idea of them, and there was Storr Peterson — the most disturbing man she had ever met.

ONE ENCHANTED SUMMER
Anne Tedlock Brooks

A tale of mystery and romance and a girl who found both during one enchanted summer.

CLOUD OVER MALVERTON
Nancy Buckingham

Dulcie soon realises that something is seriously wrong at Malverton, and when violence strikes she is horrified to find herself under suspicion of murder.

AFTER THOUGHTS
Max Bygraves

The Cockney entertainer tells stories of his East End childhood, of his RAF days, and his post-war showbusiness successes and friendships with fellow comedians.

MOONLIGHT
AND MARCH ROSES
D. Y. Cameron

Lynn's search to trace a missing girl takes her to Spain, where she meets Clive Hendon. While untangling the situation, she untangles her emotions and decides on her own future.

NURSE ALICE IN LOVE
Theresa Charles

Accepting the post of nurse to little Fernie Sherrod, Alice Everton could not guess at the romance, suspense and danger which lay ahead at the Sherrod's isolated estate.

POIROT INVESTIGATES
Agatha Christie

Two things bind these eleven stories together — the brilliance and uncanny skill of the diminutive Belgian detective, and the stupidity of his Watson-like partner, Captain Hastings.

LET LOOSE THE TIGERS
Josephine Cox

Queenie promised to find the long-lost son of the frail, elderly murderess, Hannah Jason. But her enquiries threatened to unlock the cage where crucial secrets had long been held captive.

THE TWILIGHT MAN
Frank Gruber

Jim Rand lives alone in the California desert awaiting death. Into his hermit existence comes a teenage girl who blows both his past and his brief future wide open.

DOG IN THE DARK
Gerald Hammond

Jim Cunningham breeds and trains gun dogs, and his antagonism towards the devotees of show spaniels earns him many enemies. So when one of them is found murdered, the police are on his doorstep within hours.

THE RED KNIGHT
Geoffrey Moxon

When he finds himself a pawn on the chessboard of international espionage with his family in constant danger, Guy Trent becomes embroiled in moves and countermoves which may mean life or death for Western scientists.

TIGER TIGER
Frank Ryan

A young man involved in drugs is found murdered. This is the first event which will draw Detective Inspector Sandy Woodings into a whirlpool of murder and deceit.

CAROLINE MINUSCULE
Andrew Taylor

Caroline Minuscule, a medieval script, is the first clue to the whereabouts of a cache of diamonds. The search becomes a deadly kind of fairy story in which several murders have an other-worldly quality.

LONG CHAIN OF DEATH
Sarah Wolf

During the Second World War four American teenagers from the same town join the Army together. Forty-two years later, the son of one of the soldiers realises that someone is systematically wiping out the families of the four men.

THE LISTERDALE MYSTERY
Agatha Christie

Twelve short stories ranging from the light-hearted to the macabre, diverse mysteries ingeniously and plausibly contrived and convincingly unravelled.

TO BE LOVED
Lynne Collins

Andrew married the woman he had always loved despite the knowledge that Sarah married him for reasons of her own. So much heartache could have been avoided if only he had known how vital it was to be loved.

ACCUSED NURSE
Jane Converse

Paula found herself accused of a crime which could cost her her job, her nurse's reputation, and even the man she loved, unless the truth came to light.